Mack kissed her abruptly...

...and Eliza went absolutely still, her heart taking over the rapid rhythm of her nervous chatter. He was kissing her to shut her up. She knew that. But the feel of his mouth on hers was magical, and her breath caught in helpless wonder.

When his lips moved against hers, it took a moment for her to realize he was whispering. "Don't panic, but he's got a gun. We're being kidnapped."

His words had to battle upstream against a riot of impulses slugging it out in her brain. *Kiss him back. Don't panic. Kiss... Kidnapped?* She struggled to sit up, but he wouldn't budge.

"Did you hear me?" His dark eyes stared into hers, frustration, fear, and angry determination shining clearly from their depths. "We're being kidnapped."

She realized the limo was in motion. "Why?" she whispered back. "Why kidnap us?"

He gave her a look of skeptical and utter disbelief. "It's the dress, Eliza. Chuck wants the million-dollar dress."

Dear Reader,

Magic, like love, is in the eye of the beholder. So who's to say that magic, along with love, can't be stitched into the seams of a wedding dress…an antique gown that changes the lives of three special brides and their unsuspecting bridegrooms. I imagined just such a dress and the mischief that might occur if someone other than the intended bride put it on. In *Million-Dollar Bride*, mischief is exactly what happens when Eliza Richardson tries on the magic wedding dress and her destiny collides with that of MacKenzie Cortland.

Daydreamer that I am, I believe it could happen, and as you read Eliza and Mack's story, I hope you will believe it, too. After all, isn't there a touch of magic, a gentle twist of fate, anytime a man and woman fall in love?

Sincerely,

Karen Toller Whittenburg

Karen Toller Whittenburg

MILLION-DOLLAR BRIDE

Harlequin Books

TORONTO • NEW YORK • LONDON
AMSTERDAM • PARIS • SYDNEY • HAMBURG
STOCKHOLM • ATHENS • TOKYO • MILAN
MADRID • WARSAW • BUDAPEST • AUCKLAND

ISBN 0-373-16621-4

MILLION-DOLLAR BRIDE

Copyright © 1996 by Karen Toller Whittenburg.

Printed in U.S.A.

Chapter One

The garment bag contained a million dollars, and Eliza could hardly wait to get her hands on it. So the moment Mrs. Pageatt walked, stiff as a starched crinoline, around the corner and out of sight, Eliza locked the door of the Marry We Go Bridal Boutique and flipped the sign in the window to Closed.

Desperate situations called for desperate measures, and Eliza figured she had thirty minutes, probably more, before Mrs. Pageatt returned from her appointment. Even if she came back earlier than expected and found the door locked, Eliza was sure she could explain. She was very good with explanations.

She wasn't so good at picking locks, however, and getting into the storage room took ten precious minutes. But finally she faced the garment bag, her pulse thundering. She'd never seen a million dollars. Never been this close to anything worth even half that much money. Her fingers trembled a little as she reached for the zipper.

"You have got to be kidding," she said aloud, pushing aside the garment bag and getting her first full view of the wedding gown it had held. She frowned. She stepped close and squinted. Stepped back and stared. Walked in a slow circle around the dress and then squinted some more. But her initial impression remained a flat disappointment. She wouldn't have paid ten dollars for this dress, much less a million, plus tax.

And to think she'd schemed, plotted and connived for a chance to see it. She was risking her job just being in the same room with it. And for what? There was nothing special about this bridal gown, nothing remotely exciting. Nothing that sparked her imagination or fired her creative zeal. She had thought that seeing the dress would enkindle ideas for her own designs. She had thought if she could just touch a dress that was actually worth a fortune, then somehow her own future as a designer would be assured. From the first moment she'd heard about it, she'd imbued the dress with magical properties, spun a dozen romantic fables around its mysterious past, wasted more than one evening doing sketches of what it might look like.

But as usual, her imagination had run amok, and now she was faced with this disappointing reality. No wonder Mrs. Pageatt hadn't wanted anyone to go near the storage room. No wonder she'd gone out of her way to protect the illusion that this dress was more valuable than any other.

"The gown is a Worth, my dear," Mrs. P. had said in her tight, highborn tone. "He designed it at the turn of this century, and through a series of fortuitous circumstances, it has come to me in perfect—absolutely mint—condition. I'd wager my diamond bracelet that the dress has never even been worn. In fact, I would not be at all surprised to learn that it was placed in that bank vault the very day it arrived in this country from France. You, Eliza, being a member of the *younger* generation, cannot fully appreciate the quality of craftsmanship, the simplicity of design, and as to having a sincere regard for its value... Well, I'm afraid I have to tell you, my dear, a gown like that is simply above your touch.''

Eliza narrowed her gaze on the wedding dress and decided that if this dress was above her touch, there wasn't much point in reaching any higher. In the cool shadows of the storage room, the Worth gown didn't look valuable. It looked old, faded and rather drab.

Maybe if she brought it out into the light, she could figure out what had prompted a rich California movie producer to purchase it for his daughter. If he had wanted the dress for a movie, as a costume piece, she could have understood. But if he thought a modern California girl was actually going to wear *this* dress for her wedding, he was several frames short of a full reel.

With a shake of her head, Eliza lifted the dual hangers and carried the dress into the well-lit and multimirrored dressing room. She stripped away the protective paper that clung to the hem and stood back to examine the dress once more. Carefully, she studied the blend of smooth satin and textured lace. She evaluated the hint of ivory in the material, inventoried the detail in the beadwork and absorbed the overall effect of the dress. Better, she thought. But still hardly worth a cool million.

Eliza stepped onto the platform before the wide, triple mirror and held the dress against her body, turning from side to side, trying to find the elusive quality that made this wedding gown such a prize. But no matter which way she turned, the dress looked disappointingly ordinary. She hoped Mrs. Pageatt had already cashed and deposited the check in a secret

Swiss bank account, because when this gown arrived in California...

She fluffed the skirt and checked the result in the mirror. Dismal. In the interest of being fair, she supposed she ought to try it on.

Often a gown on a hanger would be sorted over, passed by, deemed pretty, but not special. Then a bride-to-be tried it on and somehow, in some inexplicable manner, all the parts became something more than the whole and the effect was altogether stunning. She had seen it happen dozens of times during her tenure as Mrs. Pageatt's underpaid and overworked apprentice.

On the other hand, if that same apprentice got caught with the dress on...

Pursing her lips in indecision, Eliza drew the satin skirt to her waist and held it in place with her arm. She cocked one hip and then the other, setting the gown in motion, watching as the fabric shifted into deep, ivory folds, revealing a glimpse—merely an enticing hint—of hidden attractions. Temptation floated around the room like a bit of lint, landed on Eliza's shoulder and stuck fast.

The storage room was already open. The dress was already out of the bag and in her hands. She was a dead duck in or out of the dress, anyway, so she might as well put it on. As her Auntie Gem would say, "In for a penny, in for a pound."

Before her next thought—that Auntie Gem's wisdom was often flawed—could stop her, Eliza was already stripping off her serviceable cotton jumper and stepping out of her Old Maine Trotters. The buttons tacked every quarter of an inch down the back of the wedding gown slipped efficiently and easily from the satin-fabric loops, and Eliza had to admire the construction of the gown even as she slipped it over her head and gently worked her hands through the delicate lace tunnels that formed the sleeves. Someone had spent hours making this dress, stitching every seam by hand, sewing by gaslight or candlelight or maybe only by sunlight. There was love in this dress, and pride, and more than a thread of someone's hopes and dreams.

All right, she thought. So the gown was worth a few thousand...even if it wasn't exactly breathtaking. It felt good—sleek, slippery and cool against her skin. The lace was an airy network of silk encircling her arms, and the satin skirt rustled, making a whispering sound that was soft and lush and satisfying.

Postponing the showdown between fantasy and reality, she closed her eyes as she reached behind her back and, one by one, fastened the dozens of tiny buttons that ran from her hipline to the center of her back, then skipped a wide swath of lace and held the dress at her neckline. Once the back was fastened, she had to open her eyes—just a slit, though—so she could see how to slip the satin loops over the row of tiny satin-covered buttons on each sleeve, below the elbow to the wrist. Once that was done, she squeezed her eyelids tightly shut again, gave the skirt a series of gentle twists, adjusted the fall of the train in back, and then, taking a deep breath, opened her eyes for the first, expectant look in the mirror.

Her lips parted in surprise. She blinked once and then again. This couldn't be the same dress. She couldn't be that enchanted-looking woman. Something must have gotten switched somewhere, because this dress, this inspired creation of Irish lace and ivory satin, was worth every penny of a million dollars, plus every dime of luxury tax. On the hanger, the gown had looked lifeless and outdated, listless and ordinary. But now, inexplicably, *something* had changed....

She raised her shoulder and the fabric shifted with an undercurrent of energy. She touched the skirt and the satin rippled like vanilla ice cream melting on a cone. She made a quarter turn and the gown flowed, catching the light, awakening like a new day. Personality shimmered in the folds of the rich, heavy satin, glistened in the lustrous pearls strung on the silver threads across the bodice, winked like a vein of gold in the delicate spidery lace.

Unable to take her eyes off her astonishing reflection, Eliza reached for the veil, which was still draped over a hanger. Her experienced fingers automatically fluffed the netting as she set the lackluster concoction of lace and satin rosettes on her head. The transformation was instantaneous and amazing. The headpiece matched the dress, not only in style and material, but in the mystical way it completed the picture. It was lace and satin, sparkle and enchantment, a gossamer circlet around her head. She stared at her reflection, knowing that if life were a fairy tale, Prince Charming would walk into the bridal shop at this precise moment.

The moment passed and she sighed. Even if Prince Charming arrived at the bridal shop right now, he'd find the door locked and the shop closed. Timing was the reason she, plain Eliza Richards, looked breathtakingly beautiful in a dress that no one else would ever see her wear.

Deciding she might as well enjoy the moment, she turned slowly and admired herself from every angle, even twisting her neck so she could look over her shoulder and see the bustle and train. No matter which direction she turned, the fabric draped in flawless folds, the hem floating a bare quarter inch from the floor. It was uncanny how well the dress fit. If she had been the million-dollar bride, the gown wouldn't have required any alteration. Not a single stitch.

Eliza made a face in the mirror. She wasn't the bride. She wasn't even the bridesmaid. She was just a clerk in a bridal shop, with dreams that were bigger than her prospects and with an imagination that defied reality.

Distant thunder rumbled, then faded, and she took it as a ten-minute warning. Mrs. Pageatt could return anytime now and she didn't want to be caught staring at herself in the mirror. She didn't want to be caught at all. Not that Mrs. P. would murder her or anything—at least, not while she was wearing the dress.

As she turned to the mirror for one last look, her heart leapt in alarm. There was a man standing behind her, his image reflected as clearly in the mirror as her own. She had an instant impression of arrogance and kindness, of self-sufficiency and need, of a man who laughed easily, but not often. She knew that he was taller and older than she, but not by much on either count. She could see the lines of character in his face and the set of determination in his jaw. And she could tell, somehow, that he was as lost in his world as she was in hers.

The knowledge held her motionless, and she could do nothing but stare into the reflection of his eyes as he stared into the reflection of hers. Captured like a wisp of smoke in a bottle, she stood for what could have been a lifetime or a heartbeat while a thousand

promises broke open inside her and vanished before
she could name them.

Abruptly aware of a belated sense of danger, she
spun on her heel to face the man...and met only
emptiness. There was no one in the brightly lit dressing room but her. Turning again to the mirror, she saw
no reflection but her own. She stared, wide-eyed and
unblinking, but not even a hazy shadow could be seen
in the glass. Nothing but the rather forlorn image of a
bridal-shop clerk in a dress she could never hope to
afford.

"Snap out of it," she said briskly to reassure her
racing pulse. There was no one else in the shop, no
sound except the air conditioner's hum and the occa-
sional thunder roll. Her imagination had produced a
Prince Charming to match the wedding gown, an image to parallel her fantasy. Already, she'd forgotten
what he looked like...although if she put her mind to
it...

"Give your imagination an Academy Award and get
on with your life, Eliza." Tipping her head to one side,
she cast one final, luxurious, full-length look at herself in the million-dollar bridal gown. "Get out of the
dress," she continued aloud. "If your imagination
doesn't kill you, Mrs. Pageatt most assuredly will."

The words had no sooner warmed her lips when she
realized she had a problem. She couldn't imagine how
or when it had happened, but a button on the left
sleeve had snagged the lace of the bodice, tieing her
wrist to her waist. She moved her hand and felt the
grip of the lace as it pulled taut. Immediately, she
stopped, and the pressure on the snag eased.

Frowning, she assessed the possibility of damage as
she used her right hand to smooth the pucker of fab-

ric around the button. She wiggled the button to no avail, picked at a thread in the lace, tugged at the tangle, and nearly had a heart attack when she heard a tiny ripping sound.

Gulping in a deep, panicked breath, she soothed the lace with her fingertips and looked for the damage. But the only problem she could see was the button, still caught in the bodice lace. *It's all right,* she thought. It hadn't torn. There was no need to panic. She could fix this. She was very good at mending, and this was only a minor tangle... as tangles went. All it needed was a little patience, a dab of TLC, a measure of calm, clear-headed concentra—

She froze at the unmistakable and riveting sound of the shop's bell. As clear as a death knell, Mrs. Pageatt's voice followed the cheerful jingle. "Eliza? Eliza? The door was locked. Oh, Eliza?"

Like a barrage of advancing tanks, the sound of her own name bombarded the back room where she stood, nailed dead to rights, as guilty as sin, caught like a thief with her hand in the till. She frantically composed an explanation.

"Eliza?" There was the irritating clamor of the bell as the front door closed and then the *click, click, click* of Mrs. Pageatt's heels on the tiled entrance.

To hell with explanations. She was getting out of sight as fast as possible. She scooped up the skirt, draped the satin train over her immobilized arm and ran barefoot from the room. Past the line of fitting rooms, she ran like a mouse scurrying for cover. Past rows of lustrous taffeta and textured silks in the bridesmaid's boutique, past the alteration station and between the racks of ready-to-be-dyed shoes. Artfully dodging a box of heart-shaped potpourri, she saw the exit sign above the alley door and knew she was home free. Well, not free exactly, but if she could just get outside, just have a minute or two to think about what to do next...

"Eliza?"

Mrs. Pageatt was coming around the front counter toward the back. Eliza could tell by the sound of the woman's voice, her own name moving closer and closer. She grabbed for the doorknob with her free hand, shoved back the metal bolt and slammed her hip against the door all at the same time, pushing her way outside into the alley and pulling the door behind her. It closed with a clank, and she figured she had three, maybe four minutes at most to get that pesky button—

Plop! Plop-plop! In quick succession, raindrops splattered like small disasters all around her. She raised her frowning face to the grumbling sky and got hit in the eye by another drop of precipitation. Twenty percent chance of light showers in the Kansas City area, the weatherman had said on the noon news. Trusting soul that she was, she didn't even own an umbrella. She didn't have insurance, either—at least none that would cover the accidental drowning of a million-dollar gown.

"Every cloud has a silver lining." She quoted Auntie Gem, even though things looked pretty bleak at the moment.

Then, like a knight on a white steed charging to her rescue, a long, silver-gray limousine turned into the alley from the connecting street. It drove straight toward her, then veered into the parking lot several yards from the doorway where she stood. The limousine stopped, its motor idling, half in, half out of the alley, its nose forward, like a thoroughbred at the starting gate.

The driver's door opened and a burly man dressed as a chauffeur stepped out. He leaned forward to converse with someone inside the limo, then closed the door with a single shove and walked quickly out of sight, toward the front of the boutique.

A raindrop struck Eliza's head dead center, dampening her hair encircled by the satin rosettes and lace veil. "Faint heart ne'er won fair lady," she whispered. Then, with her free hand clasping the headpiece and her trapped hand clutching the bunched skirt, she ran for the limo and the opportunity fate had so thoughtfully provided.

Chapter Two

Mack wished he'd thought to request a decent bottle of Scotch. Though the rented limo came equipped with an assortment of liqueurs, there wasn't a good Scotch among them. Pushing back the sleeve of his tux, he checked his watch. Ten of three. Too early for a drink. Too late now to avoid *being* late for the three-o'clock wedding. Canon in D was resounding in the halls of St. Pat's at this very moment. Leanne was already there—had probably been there for hours—dressed and waiting, calm, composed and undaunted by the news that her bridegroom had yet to arrive.

He leaned his head against the leather seat, knowing she would wait ten minutes or ten days for him to arrive at the altar. In one way or another, he supposed, she'd been waiting for him most of her life. Still, it was inexcusable of him to be late.

The rain picked up its tempo with a random *ping, ping-ping* against the roof, and Mack wondered if most bridegrooms felt this same odd mix of resignation and resistance. Of course he wanted to get married. It was the right time for him to make such a commitment, and Leanne was the perfect choice as his wife. They knew the same people, liked the same activities and traveled in the same social circles. Her family was as conservative as his and every bit as proper. In many respects, she was better suited to bear the Cortland name than he was. His feeling of emotional doors slamming shut inside him had to be a normal, last-minute reaction. After all, they had been planning this wedding for nearly three years, and in an hour it would be over.

Suddenly, the door jerked open and a bride scrambled into the seat across from him. Her backside landed at an awkward angle and her bare feet, with rosy-tipped toes, made a smooth arc in the air as she rolled and then settled into a more-or-less-upright position. She didn't even pause for breath before she lunged for the door handle and, with a fussy rustle of ivory satin, yanked the layers of her skirt inside the car a mere second ahead of the slamming door. She held her left hand cradled close to her waist like a broken wing as she acknowledged him with a careless and fleeting glance. "Hello. This will only take a minute," she said in a rush.

Mack couldn't decide how to respond. Should he ask the obvious—*what* was only going to take a minute? Or should he wait politely for her to leave? He leaned back against the leather seat and studied her, wondering whether she was running to a wedding or away from one.

In her flustered condition, she was attractive...in a haphazard sort of way. Her long, dark hair was rumpled, as if it hadn't been combed since she'd gotten out of bed, and the damp curls on top of her head skewed over, under and around the headpiece that looped her forehead. Her makeup was careless, maybe even nonexistent, and she didn't look old enough to get a marriage license without her mother's consent.

His gaze dropped to the full, heavy thrust of her breasts beneath her bodice and he added a few years to his initial impression. Not that a few years either way mattered...because there was something about her that warned him to run like hell in any direction she wasn't going.

He watched with frank curiosity and waited for her to say something by way of explanation, but her whole focus was on smoothing the folds of her skirt and adjusting the position of her arm. She fussed with it continually, in a kind of frenzied self-control.

"Are you all right?" he asked finally.

"Not yet, but a minute either way could make the difference."

He frowned and studied the dark crown of hair ringed by the old-fashioned circlet of off-white roses, which was all he could see of her head. He ventured a guess. "Runaway bride?"

"Million-dollar dress," was her mumbled and unfathomable answer.

"Is that a yes?"

He suddenly found himself facing a pair of honest gray eyes that viewed him with startled distraction. "Look, I know this probably seems strange and all, but if I don't get out of this dre—" Thick, straight lashes blinked up and her distraction vanished, replaced by a hesitant but dawning recognition. "Wait a minute. I know you...don't I?"

Was she trying to pick him up on the way to his own wedding? Or on the way to hers? "I don't think so," he said, in his best I'm-not-interested, better-luck-elsewhere tone.

Her answering smile was friendly and unfazed. "Oh, yes, I do. I do know you."

"I sincerely doubt that we've ever met." Actually, he was quite certain of it. He had a knack for avoiding trouble, and this woman—no matter how innocent distracted or otherwise occupied she looked—was trouble on the hoof. Bare hooves, in her case. "I don't see how I could have forgotten you."

She wrinkled her nose in a charming display of candor. "Oh, don't worry. People do it all the time. I guess I just kind of blend in with the wallpaper or something."

For her, blending into the background was clearly impossible, and he decided she expected him to contradict her. So he didn't. "I have a good memory for faces."

She laughed, a natural, spontaneous sound that somehow enhanced his uneasiness. "Oh, faces." She waved her hand in dismissal. "I'm not always good with faces, but I'd know that suit anywhere. Waist, thirty-four. Inseam, thirty-five. Coat, forty-six. Shirt, sixteen. Sleeves, thirty-four and a quarter. Shoes, eleven, D." She smiled, pleased. "I can spot one of our tuxedos at forty paces."

"*Our* tuxedos? Do you *work* here—at the boutique?"

Her smile vanished and her gaze dropped like a rock to her wrist. "Well, I did when I woke up this morning."

He told himself not to ask. He did not need to know.

She told him anyway. "Let's just say I think I'm on probation at the moment."

He looked purposefully at his watch. She bent her head and fussed with a button or something at her waist. It was hard to tell what she was doing, and whatever it was, he did not want to get involved.

"You know, you literally saved my life by driving in here when you did."

This was trouble. He could feel it. "Merely a coincidence." He wanted to avert any idea she might be forming that he had meant to rescue her. "My vest had a stain. The limousine driver's inside the shop picking up a replacement right now."

"Oh, Mrs. Pageatt won't like that."

"The stain or the limo driver?"

"Whichever is uglier. She's very particular about how things look."

"It's only a small stain."

"Try explaining that to Mrs. P." Her brow furrowed with worry as she plucked at the lace encircling her wrist. "Oh, drat! I just can't get this untangled."

She lifted troubled gray eyes to his, and he steeled himself to resist their unspoken plea. Unfortunately, she didn't leave it unspoken.

"Could you . . . ?" she asked. "Would you mind giving me a hand?"

It was no wonder the Age of Chivalry had died, he thought. With a quiet sigh, he resigned himself to the inevitable and asked, "What seems to be the problem?"

The sound of a siren wailed far down the street, and her head jerked up so fast that the headpiece slipped forward and settled on the bridge of her nose. She shoved it back to her hairline and swatted at the flutter of veil as she looked, wide-eyed, out the window, then back at him. "What problem?"

"The one you're having with your dress."

She followed his gaze to her wrist. "Oh, that. Yes. Well, I have no idea how this happened . . . but my sleeve is caught and I just can't seem to get it *un*-caught." She glanced out the darkly tinted side window. "Can anyone see in here?"

His eyebrows went up. What the hell was keeping Chuck? "I don't think so, no. Is someone . . . looking for you?"

The headpiece rose a quarter inch on her furrowed brow. "Why would anyone be looking for me?"

Her denial was too fast, her voice too high, clearly indicating that someone *was* looking for her—or ought to be. "I don't know," he said. "You seem a little distraught, that's all."

The siren got louder, and she shot another anxious glance toward the window. "I'm not distraught. I'm just tangled up."

Not that he had much experience, but she certainly seemed to be acting like a runaway bride. "Is this a last-minute case of cold feet?"

She was struggling with the button and the lace again and didn't look up. "Cold feet, wet feet or webbed feet, any way you look at it, I'm a dead duck unless I can get this button undone in the next few seconds."

"Here." He scooted forward on the seat and tried to figure out what was wrong with her wrist. He leaned forward and grasped her arm, seeing in an instant that she was, indeed, tangled up. He prepared to administer a quick jerk and break the connection between lace and button, but she slapped his hand.

"Are you *nuts?*" Her wide gray eyes accused him of treason. "Do you know how much this dress cost?"

"I thought you wanted to get free."

"I do, but not if you're going to tear it."

He glanced at his watch. "Look, do you want my help or not?"

"Yes, but...be careful," she said. "If anything happens to this dress..."

"You're a dead duck, I know." He changed seats and sat beside her. He turned her wrist carefully so he could get a closer look at the problem. Her fingers rested trustingly in his hand, and he felt an unexpected rush of protective warmth toward her. He ignored it. "There, I think I see the problem.... Yes, that's it. Hold still...."

Like a bat out of hell, a police car wheeled past the parking-lot entrance and squealed to a stop in front of the boutique. Eliza jerked forward and stared out the front windshield.

"Sit still!" Mack commanded.

"It's the police," she reported in rapid staccato. "Two of them. Getting out. Running toward the shop. Oh, dear."

"Why didn't you sit still?" Exasperation flooded him. "Now look what you've done."

She turned to face him, then looked down at the strands of lace looped like a sailor's knot around the button at her wrist, and now also wrapped around the button of his shirt cuff, just visible beneath his jacket sleeve. "How did that happen? I thought you were going to be careful."

He pursed his lips in a fierce grimace. "I'm the guy who was just sitting here, minding his own business. *You* barged in. *You* asked for help. All I asked you to do was to *sit still.*"

"But the police are here."

"Good. Maybe they can get us untangled."

She looked nervously out the tinted window. "This is going to be really difficult to explain."

"What is there to explain? It's obvious that we're stuck!"

"Yes, well, it's a bit more complicated than that."

He'd had a feeling it would be. "Look, I'll try to do this gently, but the only way to get out of this mess is to break the—"

"We are not tearing so much as a thread of this dress." She raised a pair of determined eyebrows and lifted her pert and pointed little chin. "There's a way to do this without sacrificing the gown. I just haven't thought of it yet."

"As soon as Chuck gets back out here, I have to leave for the church, so think fast."

Her sigh was tremulous and troubled, and Mack was suddenly, intensely, aware of their closeness and of her enticing scent—and of a nagging inclination to put his arm around her. Bad idea . . . even if his arm wasn't tied up at the moment.

"How much time do we have?" she asked.

"He should be back any minute."

"No, I meant how long before your wedding?"

He took a turn at glancing out the window. "Three minutes, more or less."

She bent her head over their hands, then snapped her gaze back to his. "Three minutes? Three *minutes?*"

"You heard correctly."

"How can you be late for your own wedding?"

"I'm not late. There's still time."

"Oh, right. As if you could get to the church and down the aisle in three minutes. Two and a half by now."

"Wedding ceremonies always start late."

"No, they don't."

"Yes, they very often do."

"I've been to dozens of weddings that didn't start late."

"I've been to dozens that did."

Her lips tightened in denial. "Mine won't."

"Would that be the wedding you're running away from?"

"What gave you that idea? Oh." She plucked at the skirt with her free hand. "You think I'm a runaway bride because of the dress. But I'm not. I mean, I'm not a runaway bride. I just look like one because I tried on the dress and Mrs. P. came in and...well, it's a long story. However, I assure you that when I *do* get married, my bridegroom will not be late for the ceremony."

He flexed his hand. "You can't be sure of that."

"Yes, I can. I mean, this is the way I look at it. You've waited all your life to meet this one special person, right? So, why would you take even a remote chance on being late for the ceremony that means you can be with that person for the rest of your life? It doesn't make sense."

"That isn't the way I see it."

"I'll bet she would agree with me."

"Who?"

"Your fiancée."

"I assure you, the question won't come up."

"You mean she's not going to ask you why you're late?"

He stared at her and felt a spot of sympathy for whatever bridegroom eventually married this bride. "She won't ask," he said with finality.

"Why would she marry someone she doesn't care enough about to ask why he's late for their wedding?"

"She *won't* ask."

"Will she be at all curious about me?"

He raised his eyebrows.

"Won't she think it's a little odd when you arrive at the church with me attached to your cuff?"

That was a staggering thought. "No, no, no. That is definitely not going to happen. One way or another, we will sever this connection before then."

"I think we'd better, because I'm not sure I could explain this."

"Just get us untangled."

"I'm trying." She poked at the thread with her fingernail. "I have to think about it, you know."

"I suggest you think a little faster."

She gave his wrist a sharp pinch. "Oh, sorry," she murmured with obvious insincerity. "Let's switch places."

"I fail to see how that will help."

Her eyes flashed her not-so-subtle annoyance. "Do you *want* to arrive at the altar sporting an extra bride as a cuff link?"

"Do I look like an idiot?"

"Then on the count of three, move your assets.... One, two, three." Clamping her free hand over his wrist to keep it steady, she pushed herself to her feet.

Mack did the same and the two of them stood in the car, scrunched like Japanese lanterns while they shuffled around each other like two crawdads in a fish-bowl.

"Wait! Go to your...left."

He eased to the left.

"No, right! Go right."

He retraced his step and moved right, feeling the tension on his shirtsleeve increase. Maybe the damn thread would break on its own.

"Stop! If we keep this up, the dress is going to tear for sure."

He let his gaze wander casually to hers, and knew by the tightening of her fingers against his wrist that she had read his mind. "Don't even think about it," she warned. "I have an idea. Now, you stand still and I'll move around you...."

Like a flamenco dancer with one arm tied to her waist, she eased to her left, turning, twisting, never taking her hand from its protective position, never so much as drawing a quivering breath of awareness. As for him, he was fighting a variety of insights...none of them appropriate for a man who was less than a half hour away from being a husband.

"There! I think we did it."

His hopes mingled with a curious regret. "You got it untangled?"

She frowned at him as if he hadn't been paying attention. "We switched places," she said. "That's a start. Now, sit down. Easy.... Easy.... Careful.... Careful...."

Coordinating their movements, they sat down, side by side and—as impossible as the idea had seemed a couple of minutes ago—closer together than before.

"Now, let me look at this again...." Her head bent over the twisted fabric once more, and he noted the striking contrast of her dark hair against the ivory headpiece.

"Uh-oh."

The rain cut loose, pounding the metal roof over his head in echoes of disaster. "Did you say...*uh-oh?*"

"That's not the worst thing I could say right now."

"What would the worst thing be?"

She shook her head. "You don't want to know."

He sucked in a calming breath and exhaled it slowly. "I'm sure you're right," he said. "I'm also sure you won't like what I'm going to do now, so don't watch." With that brief warning, he jerked his hand free...except it didn't come free. In fact, it barely moved. If anything, the restraint on his wrist felt stronger than before. "What in the hell is wrong with this?"

He bent his head for a better look just as she bent hers, and their foreheads met with an audible *whump*.

"Ouch!"

"Son of a gun!"

"You tried to tear my dress!"

"I *tried* to get loose," he said through gritted teeth. "I'm getting married in a few minutes and I am not dragging you with me to the altar."

"That's good, because I can't go with you."

"Then get out your scissors."

"Oh, right, like I carry a pair around in the pocket of whatever bridal gown I happen to be wearing. And even if I did, I wouldn't use them on this dress. I told you I'd think of something and I will. I just need a little uninterrupted time to—"

The driver's door opened, and thick, moist air rushed in, followed by Chuck, who dove behind the steering wheel and slammed the door, shutting the rain out and the humidity in. "Gawd Amighty!" he exclaimed. "Must be a freak storm. I watched the weather report at noon and the weatherman didn't say one word about..." He looked over his shoulder. "Well, well, well. What do we have here? A runaway?"

Mack didn't like Chuck's tone or the predatory look in his eye. "Did you get the vest?" he asked.

"Yeah." In one movement, the driver tossed it back and draped his arm across the top of the seat. "Hey, Mack, is this your woman?"

"No!"

"No!"

The denials collided like Roman candles, sparking Chuck's delighted grin. "Well, now, isn't this interesting? We got the bride. And we got the groom. But my question is...who's got a million bucks?"

Mack heard his unwanted companion gasp. "What did Mrs. Pageatt tell you?" she asked.

"Me? Nothin'. She didn't say nothin' to me." Chuck patted the seat back as he shifted his smile to Mack. "So what's the plan, man? Are we stayin'? Or are we goin'?"

"There's a hundred-dollar tip for you if you can get me to St. Patrick's Church in five minutes or less."

Chuck whistled. "A hundred buckareenos, huh? I guess that means we're a-goin'." He turned around and started the motor.

"No! Wait! I can't go anywhere in this dress. I have to explain—"

"Excuse me, ma'am," Chuck interrupted. "But you're gonna need to sit back, shut up and hold on."

He slammed the gearshift into drive, and the limousine shot out of the Marry We Go parking lot like a cannonball on a crash course with disaster.

Chapter Three

Eliza twisted in the seat as best she could and looked out the back window of the limousine. The police car was still double-parked in front of the boutique, its warning lights flashing across the rainy afternoon in a monotonous red-blue-red rotation. No one came running out of the shop to give chase to the escaping limousine. There wasn't even anyone on the sidewalk to witness the getaway. But it didn't matter. Eliza knew her goose was cooked.

"This is a disaster," she murmured as she watched the boutique, the police car and her future melt into the persistent downpour. "A gigantic disaster."

"Not yet," Mack said dryly. "But it's about to be. Have you got a pocketknife, Chuck?"

"Don't answer that, Chuck." Eliza twisted back around in a hurry. "Now, listen, Mr. Scissors-happy—"

"No, you listen. I'm cutting myself free. I'm sorry for whatever damage that causes to your dress, but it has to be done. Chuck? What about that knife?"

"Wait, please...." She tried to think of another option. "Maybe I can snip the button on your shirt or—or something."

"There's more involved than a snagged button. Look." He pointed to the tangle, but kept his head back to avoid bumping into hers a second time. A cautious man, Eliza concluded. A man who wouldn't burn his pancakes twice on the same griddle, as Auntie Gem would say. "Do you see how the lace of your sleeve is wrapped around the material of my sleeve?" he continued. "Cutting the button is not going to solve this problem."

"I could take off the whole sleeve," she suggested.

"That's a start."

"We'll have to figure out how to get your jacket off first."

"We're not cutting off *my* sleeve."

"Well, you can't think I'd cut off *my* sleeve. I told you this dress cost a fortune and Mrs. P. already thinks I stole it, and how can I return it with one sleeve missing?"

The curve of his lips bore little resemblance to a smile, impatient or otherwise. "I'm late for my wedding because I didn't want to show up with a stain on my vest. Do you honestly believe I'll agree to show up without a shirtsleeve?"

"I suppose that depends on how much you want to show up."

"Don't start that again," he snapped. "None of this is my fault. If you hadn't jumped in my limo *uninvited* and gotten me *ensnarled* in your predicament, I'd be—"

"Still late," she said, shrugging. "You really can't blame me for that."

"I can blame you for involving me in your petty theft, though, can't I?"

"Petty? You call a million dollars petty?"

"Give me a break. That dress isn't worth half that much...unless you've got diamonds sewn into the lining or something."

She couldn't believe he was being so obtuse. "You're impossible."

"*I'm* impossible? *You're* the one who created this whole ludicrous situation and—"

Chuck's voice sliced through the accusation. "You two may as well quit arguing, 'cause I don't carry a knife. Got a handgun in the glove box, but no knife."

"Anything sharp will do." Mack's breathing was fast and agitated. His anger pulsed through his arm and shoulder, which just happened to be pressed so closely against Eliza's that she could feel the rhythm of his heartbeat as if it were her own.

"Some Prince Charming you turned out to be," she muttered under her breath.

"I beg your pardon?"

She ignored his curt remark. "Chuck? Turn this car around immediately and take me back to the bridal shop."

"Turn this limo around and I'll sue you *and* the rental company for ruining my wedding day."

"That's not fair," she said. "Chuck had nothing to do with your being late."

"He will if he takes you back downtown. We're almost to the church now. After he drops me off, I don't care where he drops you."

She wiggled her trapped hand. "Where you go, I go. And believe me, it will be better in the long run to go back to the boutique and let me explain to Mrs. Pageatt. Then she can figure out a way to get us untangled without harming the dress or your tux."

"It's too late to go back."

"But what about Mrs. Pageatt? She'll never believe me if I don't go right back there and tell her exactly what happened."

"She's not going to believe you, now or a week from now. Hell, if we weren't trussed together like some overdressed Thanksgiving Day turkey, I wouldn't believe it myself."

"But I have to explain—"

"Not on my time, you don't. Someone at the church will have scissors, and that's where we're going."

"You're not being reasonable! It will only take a few minutes to go back, and you're already late—"

"Don't say it," he warned. "Chuck, that extra hundred is almost in your—"

Whump! Thump...thump...thump, thump, thump!

The noise was followed by a low, forceful string of colorful language from Chuck as he steered the limo to the curb and stopped. He turned to look over his shoulder. "We got ourselves a flat tire, folks. Got a spare in the back. Stay where you are and I'll take care of it." He opened the door and winked at Eliza. "We certainly want to keep that pretty dress out of the rain, now don't we?"

She thought she heard the hint of a threat in his remark, but it had been a crazy afternoon and her imagination was in fine form. "I'm not going anywhere," she said as he stepped outside.

"Oh, yes, you are." Mack's comment was clear enough, despite the pounding of the rain.

"I beg your pardon?"

"St. Patrick's isn't even a half a block from here. We'll walk the rest of the way."

"Very funny."

Mack looked at her, and somewhere deep in her heart, she trembled. "I'm not laughing," he said. "Let's go."

With a defeated sigh, she squeezed her eyes shut. "Okay." She gulped. "Go ahead and break the lace."

"I tried that already. It's going to have to be cut. Now let's go." He scooted across the seat, pulling her with him.

"You don't understand," she protested, agitated at the thought of the million-dollar dress after a thorough drenching. "I can't go out in this rain. That would be worse than trying to fix a few torn threads."

He reached for the door handle. "We'll run. On the count of three . . . one, two—"

The limo lurched and Eliza tumbled on top of Mack, knocking his hand from the door handle and flattening him between the door and the back seat. Pressed between their bodies, his hand splayed upward, one fingertip just brushing the beadwork that crisscrossed her breast, while her hand curved down toward the waistband of his trousers. An awkward blush infused her whole body, and she was grateful that the bodice of the dress was high necked and completely covered the telltale, red blotches she knew were forming across her shoulders and chest. Not that he could have seen them from this angle, anyway. Not with her chin practically resting on his lips. No, in all likelihood, his view of her was an unbecoming close-up of her nose.

She struggled to push herself up and encountered a hardness beneath her fingertips that made her pause. Maybe he wasn't paying much attention to the view up her nose, after all.

"Get up, will you?" His voice was tense, terse, and she renewed her struggle for balance against the unsettling jerks of the limo as one side was pumped up... and up... and up.

"I'm not sure I can," she said. "Not without your cooperation, anyway."

His breath warmed the underside of her chin as he gave a long and desperate sigh. "All right, on the count of three, you pull back and I'll push up. Got it?"

"Got it." She nodded and clipped his lower lip.

He ran his tongue gingerly over the injury. "What is it with you, anyway? Did you just wake up this morning and decide that today would be a good day to ruin my life?"

"I didn't even know you existed when I woke up this morning." She placed her free hand firmly on his shoulder and pushed as hard as she could. The binding at her waist and wrist stretched taut, but didn't break. "And in my humble opinion, you were well on your way to ruining this day without my assistance. It isn't like I planned for any of this to happen, you know. And I can fix everything, if you'll just give me a chance. I only need a little time to—"

"There is no... more... time." He pushed upright—at least as upright as possible given the slant of the limousine—and Eliza had no option but to lean heavily against his shoulder as he bent forward and grasped the door handle.

"Don't open the door." She tried one last plea. "The rain will completely ruin..."

The door swung open and the rain stopped.

Mack stepped out of the car and drew her out. Expecting to be bombarded with raindrops at any moment, she looked curiously at the sky... and felt a ray of warmth as a solitary sunbeam peeped through a cloudbank. Not a single raindrop fell anywhere near her, either, as Mack gathered the satin skirt, looped the train across her shoulder and tucked the rest of it through the crook of his arm. Putting his other arm around her waist, he propelled her away from the limo, lifted her over a puddle and set her bare feet on the rain-slick sidewalk.

"Hey!" Chuck's head popped up from behind the far left fender. "Where do you think you're going?"

"Damn, I forgot to leave the tip," Mack muttered. "I'll mail you the hundred!" he yelled over his shoulder as he kept on walking.

"Technically, he didn't earn the hundred." Eliza had to give a skip every third step just to keep up with Mack's long strides, but the effort did help keep her from worrying that some small portion of her bridal train was trailing through the puddles after her. "He didn't get you to the church in five minutes or less."

Mack barely glanced at her. "I'm sure he didn't *plan* a flat tire. Sometimes things don't work out the way you *plan*. Some days disaster strikes even when you don't *plan* on it."

"Yes, and sometimes the rain stops for no apparent reason."

He tossed her a frown and picked up the pace. "The church is just around the corner. We're almost there."

Her chest was beginning to hurt from breathing in so much of the moist, damp air, and she could only hope the corner wasn't too far ahead. "I am sorry about this. I didn't mean to ruin your wedding."

"It isn't ruined," he replied with total confidence. "Simply delayed a half hour or so."

He was right, of course. What was thirty minutes weighed against a lifetime of togetherness? She sighed. "She's a lucky girl."

"Who?"

"Your bride."

"Oh. Leanne. Yes, I believe she thinks so, anyway." He turned the corner and started up the steps of St. Patrick's, Eliza close by his side.

"MacKenzie Cortland!" A voice bounced down the steps like a live grenade, meeting them halfway.

Eliza's gaze skipped to the church's imposing facade and landed on the tall woman in a flowing aquamarine chiffon dress who stood at the top of the stairs, like St. Peter guarding the gates of heaven.

"Where in God's name have you been?" the woman said. "And who is that—that impersonator?"

"Good grief," Mack muttered under his breath.

"Impersonator?" Eliza said. "Does she mean me?"

"Let me handle this."

"I thought you said no one would notice that you're late."

"I said Leanne won't ask. I didn't say no one would notice."

"Ah." Eliza noticed that his pace had slowed considerably. "I think that woman up there is going to ask."

"That woman is my future mother-in-law, so let me handle this."

Eliza shrugged. "Okay, but in case you run into trouble, I'm pretty good at explaining..."

He shot her a sideways glance and stopped four steps below the aqua madonna. "Hello, Mother Bankston."

Her answering nod was regal, but her gaze settled with disconcerting fury on Eliza. "What is the meaning of this, MacKenzie?"

Eliza had never been called a *this* before and certainly never in that tone of voice. She tipped up her chin to observe this paragon of outrage . . . and by accident or unconscious design, rested the back of her head against Mack's shoulder.

Mother Bankston sucked in her breath. "I cannot believe you are so crass, MacKenzie, as to show up here holding hands with . . . that!"

Demoted to a *that,* Eliza became offended.

"Mother Bankston," Mack said with tight control. "Let's talk about this inside the church, please."

"And further humiliate my daughter? I hardly think so! There are four hundred guests in there, MacKenzie, who have all been waiting for you to arrive and imagining some horrible accident." Her chest expanded with the magnitude of the affront. "For you to show up here with that . . . that—"

"You are drawing the wrong conclusions." Mack took another step up, all but carrying Eliza with him.

Mother Bankston moved to block any further progress toward the church doors. "You are not going inside until you take your hands off that woman."

"Believe me, if I could take my hands off her, I would."

"Mack!" A new voice crash-landed on the church steps, and Eliza watched with interest as a woman wearing a classy lavender silk walked from the sheltered entrance of St. Pat's to join Mother Bankston at the top of the stairs. "Where have you been, Mack? How could you be late for your own wedding?" Her brown eyes, very much like Mack's, came to rest on Eliza. "And who is this?"

Eliza reminded herself that this was Mack's family and Mack's show. But if anyone else referred to her as a *this* or *that*, she was going to take charge of the explanation.

"It's a long story," Mack said. "And in front of the church is not the place to tell it. If we could all please go inside...?"

"Mackey, my boy!" A third voice, male, elderly and very loud, preceded a dapper, white-haired old man in a blue flannel jacket, who leaned heavily on a brass-and-black cane. "Bad manners to be late for your own wedding, Sonny." His faded, but sprightly brown eyes, an older version of Mack's, flipped to Eliza. "Very bad manners to bring along an extra bride."

"I'm not an extra—" She abruptly clamped her lips together.

"Hello, Grandfather." Mack raised his voice to a near yell and smiled politely, as if he hadn't just pinched Eliza's arm. "As I was telling Mother and Mother Bankston, I'd prefer to continue this discussion inside."

"About time, too," the old man exclaimed. "I told them you'd be here sooner or later. A Cortland never runs away from his obligations."

"Mack?" The new voice was cool, feminine and possessive, belonging to the woman who glided past the church pillars in a layered sheath of meringue white. Her veil floated behind her like a vapor, and with the dark clouds overhead and the stark shadows of the church at her back, Eliza thought this bride could have posed for a portrait of an avenging angel.

Graceful, blond and beautiful, she looked perfectly composed as she joined the others in looking two steps down at her fiancé and Eliza. "Who is that?"

Before Mack could open his mouth, Eliza thrust out her unencumbered right hand. "You must be Leanne. I'm Eliza Richards and I am really glad to meet you." Her proffered hand remained unclaimed, and she dropped it as she glanced in turn at the four unfriendly, frowning faces. "All of you," she amended. "I'm really glad to meet all of you."

There was a moment of stunned silence, as if the quartet on the steps had to grapple with the idea that she could talk. Four pairs of eyes stared at her, then the collective gaze swung to Mack. Eliza turned her head to look at him, too. "I thought you said they would understand."

"MacKenzie!"

"Mack!"

"Mackey?"

"Mack?"

Like a spinning bottle, his name made the rounds, and Eliza could see that some sort of explanation was in order. "Look," she began. "Mack didn't plan to bring me to the wedding, but everything happened so fast we didn't have time to think about appearances. Except that it was raining and the limousine had a flat and the next thing we knew you were all out here noticing that Mack was late for the wedding, even though he was sure you wouldn't ask, and—"

"Eliza." Mack's interruption was commanding and cool. His grip on her arm tightened. "Let me handle this."

"Don't bother, MacKenzie." Mother Bankston slipped a comforting arm through Leanne's. "It's perfectly obvious what has happened."

"Would you stop that mumbling?" Mack's grandfather demanded with a thump of his cane. "Speak up so we can hear you!"

"She said it's perfectly obvious what has happened," Mack's mother yelled.

"Nothing's happened," the old man yelled back. "I thought there was going to be a wedding!"

"It appears not." Mother Bankston glared at Mack as she patted her daughter's hand. "We are all so disappointed in you, MacKenzie. I never expected you to display such a lack of respect and consideration for my daughter, our family, even your own mother and grandfather. It's inexcusable and rude and—"

"Now wait a minute," Mack's mother turned to face Leanne's mother. "I'm certain Mack can explain, if we give him the opportunity to do so."

"We are not listening to a word he has to say as long as he's holding on to that—that . . ."

"Eliza," she supplied testily.

Mack's mother glanced at her. "Let go of her, Mack," she instructed.

"I can't," he answered. "We're attached."

"You're engaged to Leanne. You can't have known this girl long enough to form an attachment."

"Have you been seeing her all along?"

"Where did you meet her, MacKenzie?"

Grandfather thumped his cane. "What did she say?"

"Why didn't you tell me there was someone else?"

"How could you wait until the day of the wedding to spring this on us?"

"I can't believe you would do such a thing, Mack."

"Will you people stop mumbling and speak up?"

Eliza heard Mack's deep sigh, although no one else appeared to. She cleared her throat and pitched her voice above the cacophonous din. "Does anyone have a pair of scissors?"

"Who said that?" Mack's grandfather asked loudly in the sudden quiet. "And what did she say?"

"Excuse me." A clergyman stepped forward. "I couldn't help overhearing. Perhaps I could be of some assistance in resolving this dispute?"

"Father Placidus!" Mrs. Bankston grabbed the wide, flowing sleeve of his robe like it was a lifeline. "Yes, yes, please help us. Mack has done the most unforgivable—"

"Oh, Mack, how could you embarrass me this way?" Leanne covered her face with her gloved hands and began to cry.

Mack reached for her, but his hand was tied. "Leanne," he said. "This is not—"

Squealing tires cut through his words, and Eliza looked over Mack's shoulder in time to see the limousine careen around the corner and jump the curb in front of the church before it jerked to a stop. "Looks like Chuck got the tire changed," she said.

"It is best if this sort of thing happens before the marriage," Father Placidus said.

"What happened?"

"Will you be quiet, Dad?" Mack's mother turned from the older man to her son. "What is going on, Mack?"

"Uh-oh," Eliza said. "I think Chuck is coming after his tip."

Mack frowned and glanced down the steps, which Chuck was climbing two at a time. When he reached Eliza and Mack, he ignored the simmering discussion going on two stairs up, turned his back on the family and leaned close to Mack's ear. Eliza tried to overhear what he said, but with Mack standing between her and the chauffeur, and the other voices getting louder and louder every second, all she actually heard was, "dollar," "dress," and something that sounded like "trouble." From the stunned expression that crossed Mack's face, she assumed she'd heard the last word correctly, and from the look he turned to her, she knew how to complete the equation. Dollar plus dress plus trouble equaled dead duck.

"It's Mrs. Pageatt, isn't it?" she asked. "She's tracked me down, hasn't she?"

"We have to go with Chuck," Mack said quietly, his back straight and oddly rigid, his grip on her arm becoming painfully tight. "Don't say a word, just come with me."

"Is she in the limo?" Eliza turned with Mack and squinted at the darkened windows. "You really can't see inside from out here, can you? See, I told you we should never have left the Marry We Go parking lot."

"Get going." Chuck spoke softly, but sharply behind her, and she glanced back at him with surprise.

"Did she blame you for this, Chuck? Because I'll explain to her that it was not your fault."

"Don't talk, Eliza." Mack's tone was threatening, and his grip on her arm was a warning as he steered her down the stairs toward the waiting limousine.

"Mack!"

"Mackenzie! Where are you going?"

"If you leave now, Mack, I will never speak to you again."

"Where are you going, Mackey? Don't you know it's bad manners to run off with another gal on your wedding day?"

"Keep going." Chuck's murmur easily overrode the other commands, and Eliza wasn't even tempted to stop. Mack didn't seem to be bothered by their abrupt departure, either. She was sorry, though, that he hadn't let her finish her explanation. Then everything would have been all right.

But Mack had wanted to handle it, and he hadn't even tried that hard. She was the one who'd finally asked for the scissors. Not that anyone had paid her the slightest bit of attention. Not one of them had even called her by name. At least the Worth gown had survived intact. Mack's wedding was ruined, unfortunately, but the marriage would probably work out just fine.

A gust of wind came out of nowhere, whipping her skirt into a froth of satin, sending a sudden chill right through the fabric. As they reached the bottom of the stairs, the raindrops started again, and Mack didn't have to urge her to run. They crossed the sidewalk as thunder crackled overhead. Eliza grabbed for the handle herself, jerked open the door and scrambled inside just as she had before. Except this time, she pulled Mack in on top of her. She thought she heard someone yell, "Mack, come back here!" but she couldn't be sure before the door was slammed shut behind them.

"Whew!" she said. "Are you all right? I thought Mrs. Pageatt might be in here. I guess she's waiting for us back at the boutique. I wonder how she located

Chuck so quickly? It was probably pretty easy to find him because of the flat tire. I knew we should never have left the parking lot. Mrs. P. is a stickler for—''

Mack kissed her abruptly and she went absolutely still, her heart taking over the rapid rhythm of her nervous chatter. He was kissing her to shut her up. She knew that. But the feel of his mouth on hers was magical and her breath caught in helpless wonder.

When his lips moved against hers, it took a moment for her to realize he was whispering. ''Don't panic. But he's got a gun. We're being kidnapped.''

His words had to battle upstream against a riot of impulses slugging it out in her brain. *Kiss him back. Don't panic. Kiss him. Kidnap. Don't panic. Kiss...* kidnapped? She struggled to sit up, but he wouldn't budge.

''Did you hear me?'' His dark eyes stared into hers, frustration, fear and angry determination shining clearly from their depths. ''We're being kidnapped.''

She realized the car was in motion. ''Why?'' she whispered back. ''Why would he kidnap us?''

He gave her a look of utter disbelief. ''It's the dress, Eliza. Chuck wants the million-dollar dress.''

Chapter Four

Eliza frowned at Mack, but his somber expression didn't change. "He can't kidnap us," she whispered. "That would be a really stupid thing to do."

"You're right." He sat up, pulling her with him. "No doubt he'll quit being stupid any minute now."

"There's no need to be cynical. Maybe you just misunderstood what he said."

Mack had been adjusting the awkward position of their juxtaposed wrists, but he stopped to look at her. "I haven't understood anything that's happened in the past half hour, but there is nothing wrong with my hearing."

"Nothin' wrong with my hearing, either." Chuck turned his head and smiled at them over his shoulder. "So you two snuggle up and whisper all you want. I love to eavesdrop on private conversations. Do it all the time. Course, you'd be better off to try and catch a little shut-eye. This could be a long ride."

"This is insane," Mack said angrily.

"Where are we going?" Eliza asked at the same moment.

Chuck laughed, as if he were having the time of his

life. "Don't both talk at once, now. Ladies first. Eliza?"

She glanced at Mack, then repeated the question. "Where are we going?"

"For a drive in the country," Chuck said good-naturedly. "Your turn, Mack."

"You'll never get away with this."

The chauffeur tapped the horn. "Wrong! I'll have to ask you to put that in the form of a question."

"You can't actually think you'll get away with it."

"Hmm. I may have to ask for a judge's ruling, but I believe that is, in fact, a question, and the answer is...yes. Yes, I *do* think I can."

"But why?" Eliza scooted forward, but the movement was caught short by a sharp pull at her waist, and she dropped back against Mack's chest and felt his agitated breathing. "Why would you want to kidnap us?"

"Good question, Eliza. If you keep this up, you may make it to the bonus round by the time we get out of the city." Chuck signaled a turn, completed it, then smiled at her in the rearview mirror. "Let's see...why would I want to kidnap you. That's a tough one. I could say it's because that dress you're wearing is worth a million dollars to somebody, and I figure it's got to be worth at least a quarter of a million for me." His grin grew even wider. "And you wanna know the best part?" He laughed again, as if he couldn't believe his good fortune. "*You* stole it. They're all gonna be lookin' for you, not me."

She swallowed hard. "Mrs. Pageatt doesn't really think I stole it, does she?"

Chuck shrugged, still grinning. "I was in the shop before the policemen arrived. She wasn't exactly calm, you understand, and she kept saying she was sure you'd been planning this for days, that you must have taken the dress the moment she left, which gave you about an hour's head start. She said she'd always thought you was a little peculiar, but that she'd offer a hefty reward to get the dress back safe and sound.''

"I'll match whatever reward she's offering, if you'll take us back to the church right now," Mack said.

"She said I was *peculiar?*" Eliza couldn't believe it. After she'd worked so hard for Mrs. Pageatt, too. "Are you sure that's the word she used?"

"For Pete's sake, Eliza," Mack hissed in her ear, "is that important?" He raised his voice. "What do you say, Chuck? Double the reward money just for taking us safely back to the church. That's a far better deal than you're going to get from the FBI."

"It might be," Chuck conceded. "If I thought the FBI was going to come looking for a kidnapped dress."

"They will most definitely come looking for the two people you've kidnapped with it, however."

"Yeah," Chuck said. "That presents a problem, don't it?"

Several undesirable solutions to the "problem" ricocheted like bullets through Eliza's thoughts. Mack must have imagined a few solutions, himself, because he patted her hand. "Take us back, Chuck," he said. "It's the wisest thing to do."

"The way I see it, Mack, is if I took you back to the church, your fiancée would most likely take my gun and shoot you. Or maybe her mama would do it. But either way, I wouldn't get the bonus money."

Eliza nodded. "It would be better if you took us back to the bridal shop, anyway."

Mack glared at her and she glared back. "It would be better," she whispered.

"I don't see how," he whispered back.

"Sorry, Eliza," Chuck said. "But I agree with Mack. Going back to the bridal shop is clearly out of the question. On the other hand, going back to the church isn't an option, either. So I guess I'll just move ahead with my first plan and get out of town with the dress."

"You won't make it out of the city limits."

Chuck laughed as he tapped the horn twice. "Wrong again! Batting a big fat zero, Mr. Cortland. Eliza's wiping the floor with you in this round."

"This isn't a game." Mack lifted his head and met Chuck's gaze in the mirror.

Watching them, Eliza felt the first cold ripple of fear.

"You're going to get caught, Chuck. The police are probably already looking for this limousine. It won't have taken long for Mrs. Pageatt to put together your presence in the shop with my disappearance. And Mack's family was right there on the church steps as we left. Someone was bound to notice the license-plate number. I'm sure it's been broadcast all across the state by now."

"You're forgetting, Eliza, that you stole the dress. If the police are lookin' for anyone, it's you. And I'm betting that they're *not* lookin' for you in this limousine. As for Mack's family, I can't imagine that they're gonna be too all-fired anxious to come after him, considering how he ran off with another bride on his wedding day. Just my opinion, though. You're welcome to think what you like. But that's the way I'm callin' this ball game, folks." Chuck laughed jubilantly and tapped the horn three times in quick succession. "Three strikes, you're out! And Chuck the Champ wins a million dollars!"

"Chuck the Chump wins twenty years in Leavenworth Prison." Mack's epithet was low and pithy.

"Now, don't be a poor loser, Mack, my man." Quickly glancing at the right-side mirror, Chuck eased the limo into another lane and then accelerated onto the westbound ramp of Interstate 70. "Some days the good guys make it to the wedding and some days they just get their tuxedos in a tangle."

"You should meet Auntie Gem," Eliza muttered.

"Okay, kiddies, it's time to contemplate our destinies." Chuck held up a cassette tape. "Kick back, relax and meditate on my favorite song." He popped the tape into the deck and began to hum even before the first track started to play.

Eliza was aware of Mack's frustration. She'd have had to be brain dead not to pick up on the energy waves flowing directly from his body into hers. She was also aware of the muscular slope of his shoulder behind her head, the heat of his arm as it curved at her waist, the arrhythmic tapping of his fingers at her wrist. That they were actually in the throes of a kidnapping seemed patently unreal, despite the go-for-broke voice of Billy Joel spreading the philosophy of "Easy Money" over the stereo system.

"What are we going to do?" she whispered.

Mack looked down at her, his dark eyes made even darker with concern. "Try to get untangled, I guess. I don't have a chance of overpowering him with my right hand tied up like it is."

She sighed. "I wish I'd never even heard of this dress."

Mack just leaned his head back against the seat and closed his eyes as Chuck turned up the volume and sang along with Billy.

"I'VE NEVER SEEN such a mess."

Mack stopped contemplating avenues of escape and looked down at Eliza's bent head. The ring of satin flowers sat lopsided across her crown, anchored by sprigs of dusky hair. The lace netting was bunched and crimped by the frequent and unconscious pressure of her fingers as she pushed the veil out of her face. She'd tried to discard the entire headpiece about the time they hit Lawrence, Kansas, but despite his left-handed assistance, the satin roses refused to budge. A second attempt about forty miles farther west had only served to pull her hair and had brought tears to her eyes. So the veil remained on her head, caught by her tangled hair... just as the dress held tenaciously to the tangled fabric at their wrists.

His hand was asleep and his arm ached from fingertip to shoulder. He'd sorted through varying degrees of emotion to arrive at an angry truce with the facts as they now stood. He was for all practical purposes handcuffed to a woman he barely knew and did not want to know any better. He was being kidnapped by a chauffeur with delusions of wealth. He was being taken to an unknown destination, where who knew what kind of disaster awaited him. His wedding day was ruined. Ditto the honeymoon. He was hungry. And all because Eliza Richards had popped into his limo and his life like a bad case of poison ivy.

"I just don't see how this could have happened." Eliza's remark drifted up to him through a veil of dark hair and white lace.

"So you've said."

"Well, I don't understand it. I mean, it only took an instant for this dress to upset my whole life, and in two hours, I haven't been able to accomplish anything more than breaking three fingernails."

"It's been closer to three hours," he said. "Why don't you give it a rest?"

She shook her head and kept picking at the threads. "It's my fault you're in this limousine being kidnapped instead of at the reception celebrating your marriage. I can't stop trying to get you out of this mess."

He admired her determination, even as he marveled that she actually thought she could fix everything if she just undid the knot. Placing his left hand over her right one, he forced her to stop. "Take a break."

She leaned back, and the veil fluttered down over her face. Sticking out her lower lip, she breathed out little puffs of air in a vain attempt to blow the lace netting away from her eyes. Sighing, Mack lifted his hand and drew the veil up and back, tucking it and several silky strands of hair behind her ear. His fingers lingered for a moment against the soft warm hollow there, and he fought against a wave of overpowering protectiveness. "There," he said, abruptly dropping his hand.

She thanked him with a tiny smile. "Where are we?"

"Somewhere in western Kansas, I would think. I lost track of the road signs quite awhile ago."

"What do you think he's going to do with us?"

Mack wasn't about to be truthful with her on that one, even if this was all her fault. "Make us hitchhike back to the city," he said, shrugging. "Which, considering that my hitching thumb is out of service, may be difficult."

"We'll use my thumb," she offered. "It's free."

He didn't believe there was anything free about her. "Then what is there to worry about?"

"Going tone-deaf from Chuck's singing?"

Tone-deaf would be preferable to stone dead, but he didn't say so. Instead, he forced a wry smile. "At least he isn't doing Elvis impersonations."

"Thank you. Thank you very much." Chuck did a creditable Elvis imitation as he tossed a big grin over his shoulder. "Never count your blessings out loud, kiddies. 'Cause sure as you do, some little leprechaun will hear you and snatch your pot of gold right out from under your nose."

"Leprechauns seldom live happily ever after," Eliza interjected.

"Neither do brides and grooms," Chuck countered. "So go figure, huh?"

Eliza sank against Mack's shoulder as if all her strength had ebbed out of her. "He really thinks he's going to get away with this."

Mack had come to the same conclusion a hundred miles back and saw no purpose in denying it now.

"You'll never get this dress off me without damaging it," she challenged Chuck. "And it won't be worth two cents to you if it's torn."

Chuck's smile in the mirror remained good-natured. "Don't worry, little Liza, I'll get it off. I have everything figured out. Right down to the last knot." He adjusted the rearview mirror again, gave her a wink and picked up Michael Bolton in midballad.

Her sigh was deep and quivery.

Mack shifted position and reluctantly put his left arm around her shoulders. It wasn't comfortable and it probably wasn't much comfort, but under the circumstances, it was the only thing he knew to do.

"MAY I TAKE YOUR ORDER, please?"

Mack awakened with a start as the scratchy, unfamiliar voice penetrated his fitful sleep.

"Six burgers, three vanilla shakes. And make it snappy." The window whirred shut, punctuating Chuck's order with a renewal of silence.

They were stopped in the drive-through lane of a fast-food restaurant. Mack squinted through the windshield into the darkness, looking for a sign to indicate where in Kansas they were. But all he saw was the flashing neon letters signaling the entrance to Buddy's Burgers. In a glance, he assessed his opportunities and immediately discarded the idea of escape. Eliza was curled against his side like a child around a security blanket. Her right hand was tucked in the crook of his elbow, and her head rested heavily on his upper arm. Her breathing came in the long, low pattern of ponderous sleep, and he knew that making a move without her cooperation would get him exactly nowhere. As preposterous as it seemed, he was trapped in the back seat of a rented limousine by nothing more than a slip of a girl in a million-dollar dress.

Not that he believed the dress was worth that much money. Which brought him full circle to the unpalatable conclusion he'd arrived at fifteen minutes into the kidnapping; the dress was not the intended victim, he was. And if that were true, then it logically followed that Eliza and Chuck were in this escapade together. They had planned it and were going to hold him for ransom. It seemed the most reasonable explanation, even though the idea that wide-eyed Eliza could be a cold-blooded criminal went against his faith in the human race. Still, what else could he believe? Either she was guilty or the dress was worth a cool million.

He certainly hoped they didn't think he would bring that much in ransom. After today's scene on the church steps, he figured his family would demand payment themselves before they'd consider taking him back.

Chuck lowered his window.

"That'll be seven dollars and eighty-six cents."

Mack couldn't see the Buddy's Burger employee, but he seized the opportunity to yell, "Help, I'm being kid—"

Jerking upright, Eliza drowned out his cry with a series of startled and ear-splitting shrieks. "Aaaaah! Aaaaah! Aaaaah!"

"Eliza!"

She looked over her shoulder at Mack and shrieked again. "Aaaaaaah! Aaaaaaah!"

He clapped his left hand over her mouth and roughly pulled her back against him. She bit him.

"Ow!" He released her and waved his hand back and forth as if he could shake out the pain. "What did you do that for?"

In the front seat, Chuck smoothly covered the outcry with a wry laugh and a jerk of his head toward the backseat. "Newlyweds," he said, and handed over the money in exchange for the sack of food. "Keep the change, kiddo."

Before Mack had time to recover, the window was closing and the limousine was pulling out of the Buddy's Burgers' drive-through lane. "Way to go, Eliza." He rubbed his fingers over the smarting flesh of his palm and found some small comfort in the knowledge that she hadn't broken the skin and he wouldn't have to get a tetanus shot.

"Did I hurt you?" Her voice was quiet and penitent, but he wasn't fooled.

"Yes, and don't pretend that isn't exactly what you meant to do, either."

"I didn't. It's just that... well, you woke me up."

"Ah, please forgive me. I should have waited to yell for help *after* you'd had your nap. It was very inconsiderate of me to yell when there was a slim chance that someone might actually hear."

She looked down at her lap. "There's no need to be curt. I didn't do it intentionally. It's difficult for me to get oriented when I first wake up. You frightened me, that's all."

"Mmm-hmm."

"Mmm-hmm?" Her gaze slid to his face. "What does that mean?"

"You two want a burger?"

"No." Eliza snapped at Chuck, but didn't take her eyes off Mack. "You can't honestly believe I didn't want you to yell for help."

He shrugged. "What I believe, Eliza, is that you're in this whole kidnapping farce up to your ears."

Her mouth dropped open. "But that's ridiculous!"

"Is it?"

"Milk shake?"

"Shut up, Chuck." Eliza's cheeks bloomed with agitation. "All right, Mack, I'll take full responsibility for this . . . this— "

"Farce."

"Situation," she corrected. "I'll accept responsibility for this situation up to the point where we got snagged in my bodice, but I am definitely not in cahoots with Chuck and I am especially not involved in this kidnapping, up to my ears or otherwise!"

"I'd applaud your performance, but my right hand is all tied up and my left one is recovering from a bite wound."

"You shouldn't have put your hand over my mouth like that."

"Believe me, I won't do it again."

"Burgers aren't half-bad," Chuck said over his shoulder. "Sure you guys don't want one?"

"No, thank you." Eliza flounced in the seat. "We don't want anything from you."

"I'll take one." Mack pushed her up with him as he scooted forward and took the paper-wrapped burger.

"Here, have a milk shake, too." Chuck handed back the paper cup.

Mack barely managed to grasp the cup and hold on to the burger with one hand. "You could help me out with this, you know," he said to Eliza.

"Sorry, my hands are busy." She looked at him and the burger with distaste. "How can you eat that?"

"I'm hungry." Anchoring the milk shake between his thighs, he peeled away the paper and sank his teeth into the hamburger. "Want a bite?"

"As a last meal, that has absolutely no appeal." She turned her head and looked out the window.

He'd give her credit for knowing how to spoil a man's appetite. But he ate the tasteless burger anyway, every last crumb of it.

"One Buddy's Burger left, Eliza," Chuck said, rattling the paper sack. "Sure you don't want it?"

"Positive. But ask Mack. He can probably find room for one more."

Intentionally slurping, Mack finished off the milk shake. "Always room for another Buddy's Burger." He noticed Eliza's disgusted look, but he'd be damned if he was going to let her make him feel guilty. She was kidnapping him, for Pete's sake. And even if she wasn't, there was no reason for her to look so pious just because she chose to go hungry. "Got another milk shake?" he asked.

"Sorry, drank it myself." Chuck belched and tossed Mack the last hamburger. "Wish you'd eat that, Eliza. Restaurants are gonna be scarce for a while."

"What about a ladies' room?"

"You mean a toilet?"

She twisted uncomfortably in the seat. "That would do."

Mack stopped eating, his appetite arrested, his interest caught. If Chuck could be persuaded to stop at a service station, there might still be an opportunity to escape.

"Well, now, let's see." Chuck peered into the darkness as if he were searching for civilization. "Not much out here," he said. "But wait. What's that? Yep, Eliza, you're in luck." He guided the limousine onto the shoulder of the deserted road, got out and came around to the back door, flinging it open with a magnanimous gesture.

As he and Eliza struggled to step outside, Mack caught the glint of steel in the chauffeur's hand and cancelled his plan to make a run for it. No point in taking unnecessary chances. If by some fluke it was the dress that Chuck meant to hold for ransom, it stood to reason that the person he'd shoot at was the one who wasn't wearing it.

"But there's nothing here," Eliza said, her voice fading with desperation. "No service station. No facilities. Nothing."

"*Au contraire.*" Chuck gestured behind him, keeping the gun unobtrusively pointed at Mack. "There are three trees right over there. Pick one."

IF HUMILIATION could be measured in bank deposits, Eliza figured that in this one day she would have acquired enough to retire a wealthy woman. It took forty-five minutes and as many miles before her blush subsided to a warm memory. But it heated up again every time Mack looked at her, which he tactfully avoided doing as much as possible.

She kept her head bent over the knot, although she only gave it her token attention. "Fix it or fry it," Auntie Gem liked to say, and Eliza seriously considered ripping out the seams of the dress just to be free of this incredible, ridiculous tangle. But she couldn't quite bring herself to harm the wedding gown. Some bride somewhere was destined to wear this one-of-a-kind dress and be happy doing so. Eliza should just never have put it on.

Beside her, she felt the flexing of Mack's arms and shoulders as he tried to find a comfortable position. She straightened, too, as she'd already discovered that it was easier to move if they worked together. He cupped her elbow and tucked his left arm around her shoulder, turning her slightly away from him. Then, bracing his back against the door, he pulled her against him. "Why don't you stretch out on the seat?" he said. "Try to relax a little."

His smile was about the nicest thing that had happened to her all day, she thought, which wasn't saying much considering the kind of day she'd had. On the other hand, his day hadn't been anything to write home about, either. "You're a nice person to have along on a kidnapping, Mack. Thanks."

"You're welcome."

"If we ever get out of this limousine, I'll be happy to explain this whole mess to your fiancée."

"Leanne?"

Eliza frowned. "Isn't Leanne the one you were supposed to marry today?"

He removed his hand from her shoulder and stretched his arm across the back of the seat. "Yes," he said. "Leanne."

"Well, now that we have the name straight..." She flounced a little on the seat, ostensibly stretching her legs, but basically just mad at herself for mentioning his fiancée in the first place. "She must be pretty worried about you by now."

"I imagine she's basking in her mother's, my mother's and four-hundred-odd guests' sympathies. It isn't every day that a Bankston gets left at the altar."

"She can't possibly believe you jilted her?"

"I did jilt her."

"Well, sure, but not on purpose. She can't think you wanted to run off with me."

"I appeared on the church steps with my arm around another woman. Another bride, to add insult to injury. I left with my arm still around the other woman and I didn't even say I was sorry. Now, what would you believe?"

Eliza lifted her chin. "That you were being kidnapped."

He gave her a curious smile, and his hand absently settled the wayward veil. "You're funny, Eliza."

"Because I wouldn't automatically assume the worst about the man I had chosen to spend the rest of my life with?" She shook her head in mild reproach. "Give Leanne some credit. I'll bet she's frantic right now."

"Furious, yes, but she doesn't do frantic."

"Well, you've never been kidnapped before, have you?"

"No, but I'll bet you the rest of that leftover Buddy's hamburger that if Leanne has mentioned my name—and I'm certain she has—in the past few hours, it has been accompanied by a few pithy words not fit for polite conversation."

"Keep your burger, Mack. I'm sticking with frantic."

"You probably believe in Santa Claus, too."

"And happily ever after, as well, which is more than I can say for you." She raised her hand and pushed back the droopy headpiece. "I'm beginning to think you needed rescuing today worse than... Mack, look!"

He looked down, wondering why he'd noticed again her sweet smell... like fresh vanilla and summer roses and—

"It came undone."

The knot was undone. Their respective sleeves were free. Frowning, he flexed his wrist. "When did that happen?" he asked under his breath.

"I don't know. I just moved my hand like this and—"

Instantly, he realized she was waving her hands—*both* hands. He grabbed the left one with what he considered great presence of mind and pressed it down to her lap, taking care to keep his right hand tucked close to her waist. "Ssh." He cut his eyes to Chuck.

"Oh," she whispered. "Right."

But her smile was indiscreet. It was bound to give her away even if the sparkle of excitement in her eyes didn't. So he kissed her.

Her surprise was tangible, a soft O beneath the pressure of his mouth, a pleasing taste of hesitancy and curiosity. Her left hand crept up his chest, and he almost forgot to catch it and push it back to her lap. Her right hand immediately took the left one's place, sliding across his stomach and moving up, casting a tantalizing anticipation over his entire body, creating a paradox of suspense and certainty over what she might do next. She kissed a path to his ear and whispered, "Do you think Chuck knows?"

At the moment, he didn't know who Chuck was. He turned his head to recapture her lips and found himself with a mouthful of veil. "I doubt it," he mumbled after extracting the veil from his teeth.

Nodding, she snuggled closer. "Now we'll be able to escape."

He tried to remove his arm from her shoulder, but it kept sliding back. This had to be the strangest day of his life. First he was supposed to get married, then he got shanghaied, then he was caught in a knot and then he wasn't. "How did you get it undone?" he whispered. "I thought it was impossible."

She looked up at him, her eyes enchantingly full of possibilities. "That's the amazing thing," she whispered back. "I didn't do anything. I lifted my hand and the dress just let go."

He'd seen the knot, and there was no way short of a miracle it could have "just let go." And yet she looked as surprised as he was and ingenuously incapable of deceit. So if she wasn't in on the kidnapping, maybe there was some other explanation. There would have to be.

"Sure am glad to see you two gettin' along so well." Chuck turned down the volume on Mariah Carey and laid his hand along the seat back. "'Cuz it'd be miserable to be tied up together with somebody you didn't much care for, now wouldn't it?"

Mack's full attention shot back to his immediate problem. Now that his hand was free, he could overpower the other man and bring him to justice. But slam-dunking the driver of a moving vehicle was probably not the best way to go about it. On the other hand ... What other hand? He had to do something, didn't he?

"When are we going to stop, Chuck?" Eliza asked. "I'm so tired of being in this car."

Chuck glanced back and grinned. "Well, all you had to do was say so."

Eliza turned a puzzled frown to Mack. He shrugged and felt some small relief that he could wait until the car stopped before committing an act of heroism. "Where are we?" he asked, as if he was just passing the time and not plotting like a fiend. "Nebraska? Colorado?"

"Good guess," Chuck announced as he turned the limo off the deserted road.

For several minutes, the limousine bounced over a rough road...or maybe it wasn't a road at all. All Mack could see through the windows was a thick coating of dust. Kansas, he thought. They were still in Kansas.

"Here we are, kiddies. Home, sweet home." With a flourish, Chuck spun the wheel, and the limo circled and came to a stop. "Sit still. I'll get the door for you."

Eliza whirled to face Mack the moment Chuck got out of the car. "How are we going to do this?" she asked. "How about if you punch him while I grab the car keys?"

He grabbed her fluttering hands and forced the left one into position at her waist. "First of all, we pretend that we're still handcuffed to the dress. Then we play it cool and calm and we wait for the right opportunity. Now, when he opens the door, remember what I said...cool and calm, wait for the right minute...."

She looked out the back window. "What's he doing in the trunk, Mack?"

"Whatever it is, I'm against it." He thought fast and furiously. "Just follow my lead, okay?"

"Maybe I'll say a little prayer."

"That couldn't hurt, either."

Chuck opened the door for them. "All right, chickadees, your honeymoon nest awaits."

Mack helped Eliza out of the limo, being careful to behave as if the wedding-dress knot still held. "Where?" he asked. "Not that old—"

"Is that a barn?" Eliza interrupted. "There aren't going to be any horses in there, are there?"

"I don't rightly know, Eliza. Let's find out." Chuck moved behind them, and Mack gauged his best opportunity. The moment they started walking, he would wheel and punch. Wheel and punch. Wheel and—

"If there's a horse in there, I am not going in." Eliza spun around to make sure Chuck understood... and blew their cover in a split second of inattention. Mack realized the opportunity was now or never. He lunged for Chuck, who was quicker than he looked, sidestepping the assault before landing a neat uppercut to Mack's jaw and sending him sprawling on the ground with a loud *whuffff!*

Eliza gasped. "Mack! Are you all right?"

"Well, well, well. We did get ourselves loose, didn't we? Good work, Eliza." Chuck dropped to his knees beside Mack. "I'd decided you couldn't work it out and I'd have to do the trick myself. You didn't harm the dress any, did you?"

"No," she said. "What are you doing to him?"

Pain shot across Mack's neck as first one arm and then the other was jerked behind his back. She *was* in on this, he thought. What a stupid idiot he was to have tried to protect her.

"I'm tying him up. What does it look like I'm doing?"

"With jumper cables? You're tying him up with jumper cables?"

"That's right, darlin'. Necessity is the mother of invention, you know." Chuck pulled the noose tight around Mack's arms and clipped one set of terminal clamps to his pant legs, right behind each knee, and the other set to the seat of his tuxedo trousers.

"Son of a—!" Mack gritted his teeth as Chuck jerked him to his feet and the upper set of cables nipped him.

"Take those off of him right now." Eliza pulled back and let fly with her fist, clipping Chuck on the tip of his nose.

"Ow! You little she-devil." He grabbed her arm and twisted it behind her back with one hand while holding Mack's elbow with the other. Then he propelled them toward the dark, hulking shape of the barn. "I am here to tell you that neither one of you is my idea of a fun date. Now, we are going into this barn and you, Eliza, are gonna give me that million-dollar dress."

"You'll have to wrestle me to the ground to get it and it will get very dirty. Probably *torn* and dirty." Her chin went up. A bad sign, Mack thought, no matter whose side she was on.

"I'm not going to wrestle you, sweetheart. You'll give me the dress or I'll shoot Mr. Cortland."

Eliza gasped. "Shoot Mack? You wouldn't do that."

"Yes," Chuck said. "I would."

"But he had nothing to do with this. Really. I'm the one who took the dress. Not Mack."

"This is nothing personal. If Mack was wearin' the dress, I'd shoot you."

"But that isn't fair."

"Whoever told you life is fair was a dirty, lyin' scoundrel." Chuck shoved Mack through the open door and sent him stumbling into the musty darkness inside.

Mack managed to keep from falling—barely—and took in what he could of his surroundings before Eliza staggered after him. "No horses," she said, sighing. "I was worried about that."

"I can see where you would have been." His droll remark was lost on her, though, as she watched Chuck make a quick search of the immediate area.

She sidled up to Mack, her little chin held high. "I think we can take him," she whispered. "Let's rush him on the count of—"

"Give him the dress, Eliza." Mack turned his head to fortify the suggestion with a frown, but caught his breath. Moonlight breaking through the clouds streamed through a hole in the barn roof, spotlighting Eliza in a soft, silvery glow. Disheveled and tousled, with the wedding veil in disarray around her dark hair, she was a picture of pristine mischief and tempting simplicity. When she'd first bungled her way into the limo, he had thought in passing that neither she nor her dress was anything special. But now he could see his error.

Eliza's charm lay not so much in the tilt of her pert and perfect nose or her wide-eyed look of innocence or the determination in that wicked little chin, but in the character revealed in the way it all fit together. She was a portrait in progress, lovely in ways that changed with the reflections in her expressive eyes. With her wearing it, the dress became something more than just an old-fashioned wedding gown, and he suddenly wished there was some other way to save the day. "You look breathtaking in the dress," he said. "But it isn't worth dying for."

She turned her attention from Chuck, who was completing his investigative circling of the old barn. "Breathtaking?" she repeated softly, her eyes shining with pleasure. "You think I look breathtaking?"

"Yes."

"All right, Eliza." Chuck walked up behind her. "Take it off."

"I can't," she murmured, her eyes on Mack. "I look breathtaking."

The report of the gun slammed into Mack's chest at the simultaneous moment the bullet slammed into the ground next to his feet. The noise resounded in his ears, muting Eliza's startled scream into a surreal echo. Tension locked his muscles, and he nearly lost his balance as the cables pulled taut at his involuntary movement.

"You idiot!" Eliza spun toward Chuck. "You could have killed him."

"You know, you're right," Chuck said, grinning. "Good thing I wasn't pointing at him, isn't it? Now, get the dress off."

"I—I need . . . help with the buttons."

"I'll help," Mack offered.

"You're tied up and stayin' that way," Chuck said. "I'll do the buttons. Turn around, Eliza, and no funny business."

She looked at Mack questioningly.

"No funny business," he answered.

"No funny business," she repeated, resolutely pursing her lips and drooping her shoulders as she bent her head and began undoing the row of buttons on her sleeve.

At that moment, Mack decided that whatever her part in this drama, whatever the wedding gown was or wasn't worth, she was his ally.

Keeping his eye on the gun, he hoped that Chuck would put it down or drop it or just take his finger off the trigger. But unfortunately, Chuck proved agile and efficient at doing two things at once. As he worked his way down Eliza's back, unbuttoning each and every tiny button, he kept the gun barrel pointed at Mack, even when Mack tried to ease out of range.

There wasn't time to ease far, however, before the dress was sliding off Eliza's shoulders and falling into a deep ivory puddle around her knees. And his own priorities puddled into the awareness that she wasn't wearing anything under the dress but a matched set of very sheer, very sexy lingerie. He had expected, some-how—if he'd thought about it at all—that she would choose plain and serviceable underwear. Certainly not a delicate, see-through pattern of lace that was more provocative than practical.

"Whoa, babe, sexy undies." Chuck took her arm and helped her step out of the wedding dress. "But I don't think women ought to wear bras. Too confin-ing. Take it off."

Eliza looked startled, and Mack made an impulsive move to protect her... but Chuck noticed and raised the gun barrel to maintain the status quo. "Don't be a hero, Mack," he advised. "Stay put and no one gets hurt."

Mack watched helplessly as she unhooked the bra and dropped it onto the frothy pile of wedding gown. Her breasts were large and beautiful, and he was very sorry that she was forced to reveal them in such a way and in such a crude setting. Her embarrassment was a rosy flush that he sensed more than saw before tact-fully looking away.

"I'm surprised at you, Liza," Chuck continued, "wearing skimpy little drawers like that. Aren't they uncomfortable? You best let me have those, too."

"Wait a minute," Mack protested. "There's no need to take this any further. Take the dress and—"

The gun barrel and Chuck's gaze leveled on Mack. "Did I ask for your opinion, Cortland?"

"You don't have to humiliate her."

"She's got a great bod. Why would she be humiliated? Unless . . ." Chuck laughed and nodded. "I see your point. It isn't fair for me to take her clothes and not yours, now is it?"

"Life isn't fair," Mack said a little desperately.

Chuck shook his head. "Now what idiot told you that?"

Chapter Five

"I can't believe he was such a liar." Eliza moved her bare shoulders in an experimental wiggle...a wiggle that raced like a static charge through Mack's already overwrought nerves. They were sitting on the barn floor, naked backside to naked backside, tied together by one overextended set of jumper cables. The cable twisted securely over and around their wrists—her palms against his hips, his against hers—then circled their waists and wrapped back around their hands. The terminal clamps looped over and through to hold the double knots like bull-terrier pups clinging tenaciously to a chew toy. It was not, Mack thought, the way he had planned to spend this night.

"He had a pair of scissors in the limousine all along," Eliza continued. "A pair of scissors! Can you believe it?"

"No, I can't," he answered dutifully, even though the bare evidence was exposed to the cool night air. "Until he pulled those scissors out of his pocket and cut my tuxedo to ribbons, I thought Chuck was a real great guy."

Her pause was brief, but significant as his sarcasm

sank in. "You're right. I shouldn't be sitting here all upset because he lied to us about a pair of scissors."

"It would make more sense for you to be upset because we're sitting in a deserted barn somewhere in western Kansas without a stitch of clothes between us."

"I thought you didn't know where we were."

"I'm guessing. Does it really make any difference?"

"There's no need to raise your voice. I'm right behind you, you know."

As if he were apt to forget. The smooth feel of her bare back against his was a constant reminder of just how close she was and just how devious Chuck had been. "I thought maybe the gunshot had affected your hearing."

"Sure you did. Just like you thought I was Chuck's gun moll."

"I never called you a *gun moll,* for Pete's sake."

"But you sure thought I was in on the kidnapping, didn't you?"

"That possibility made more sense to me than your explanation that the dress was worth a million dollars."

She sniffed. "Well, now you know, don't you?"

Arguing was pointless, especially considering the awful predicament they were in. "I know we have to figure a way out of this before Chuck changes his mind and comes back."

"He's halfway to California by now." Eliza dipped her shoulder, raking Mack's upper arm with a silky friction. "We won't see him again. And I will probably never see the Worth gown again, either."

"You may never see the outside of this barn if we don't get our hands untied."

"It isn't like we haven't tried, Mack, but in this position..."

"Then we'll have to try another position and another one, and so on until we get it right." He clenched his fingers and chafed his wrists against the plastic cable...and quickly managed to pull Eliza even closer against him than before.

"Congratulations," she said. "Now I can barely wiggle my fingers."

She demonstrated, her fingertips moving like a downy glove over his bare buttocks, her touch adding a whole new dimension to his perception of this dilemma.

"See what I mean?" she continued. "I bet you can't wiggle yours, either."

Wiggling his would only make matters worse...a lot worse. "Come on, Eliza. Considering how fast you got us twisted up in that dress, surely one set of jumper cables can't pose too much of a challenge."

"As I had nothing at all to do with getting us *un*-twisted from that dress, I don't see what you think I can do with jumper cables."

"Don't be modest. You worked for hours on that tangle."

"To no avail. I'm telling you, the dress just let go."

"*After* you worked on the knot for hours," he repeated a little more forcefully. "Look, all I'm saying is that we have to keep working on these cables. We can't stay like this forever, you know."

She sighed and leaned her head against his shoulder, her hair fanning across his skin like a soft blanket. "The stars are really bright. Look. You can almost see the whole Cygnus constellation through that hole in the roof. All but the tip of the swan's wing."

He looked up. Constellation? She could recognize a constellation?

"It must be easier to see out here in the country because there aren't any streetlights," she continued. "Or city lights. There isn't much of anything out here, I guess. Except for you and me and what sky we can see through the hole in the roof."

He gave the shadowed rafters a prosaic once-over. "I wonder if anyone uses this barn."

"Tamra and Jake meet here sometimes. It's the only place they can be sure her father won't find them."

He frowned, then turned his head and tried to see Eliza out of the corner of his eye. "Who in the hell are Tamra and Jake?"

"Star-crossed lovers, I imagine."

"You imagine?"

"Well, look around, Mack. Who else would meet in a deserted old barn like this?"

"A couple of barn owls? I don't know what you're talking about. How do you know Jake and Tamra?"

She shrugged. "I don't. You wanted to know if anyone uses the barn, and those names popped into my head and I said them, that's all."

"Are you telling me you're psychic?"

He felt her answering smile in the relaxing droop of her shoulders. "No," she said. "I just made them up."

He was tied to a nut case, a real fruitcake. "Don't you have better things to think about?"

"Not unless I count how bright the stars are. We may as well face facts, and the fact is this hasn't been a banner day for blessings. I'd rather imagine some love-struck couple bringing warmth and passion into this barn than worry that no one will find us until we're dead and all shriveled up like raisins."

"Western Kansas isn't that remote, Eliza."

Her laughter was first a sly movement of her skin against his and then a soft sound in the quiet barn. "Imagine the surprise of whoever does find us. We might not be very far from civilization, but I'll bet walking into a barn and discovering two naked people wrapped in jumper cables will make somebody's eyes cross."

The image made him smile. "Maybe we'll make local headlines. Adam and Eve Found In Farmer Brown's Barn."

"Fig Leaves Loose in Pasture."

"Nude Couple Has Dead Battery."

"A Nude Use For Jumper Cables!"

He laughed with her, his tension easing with the throaty, pleasant sound of her humor. There were bright spots in this whole comedy of errors. He was alive, for one thing. Unharmed, for another. And his companion was not crying, screaming or threatening mayhem. Fruitcake or not, Eliza was easy to be with. Under similar circumstances, Leanne would have been hysterical.

Who was he kidding? Under any one of these stressful circumstances, Leanne would have been throwing a full-fledged tantrum. Certainly, she would never have imagined the dilapidated old barn as the rendezvous point for a lovers' tryst. And in a million years, it would never have occurred to her to look through a hole in the roof and locate the Northern Cross.

An oddly comfortable quiet settled over him. "Thank you, Eliza."

"For what?"

"For not making a bad situation worse."

Her head moved against his shoulder. "Do you think this situation can *get* any worse?"

His answering chuckle came more easily this time. "I guess whatever happens next will have to be an improvement."

"I agree. But frankly, I'm surprised that you feel that way. I had you pegged as one of those high-maintenance men. You know the kind—shoes polished, every hair in place, leather pocket planner with things like 'lunch with Mom' and 'tennis at club' penciled in. I would have bet twenty-three dollars and forty-eight cents that you had 'get married' written in under today's date."

"Pencil or ink?"

"Felt-tipped pen."

"It was a Mont Blanc ballpoint." He waited for her protesting laugh, which didn't come. "I was kidding, Eliza. I don't have a pocket planner."

"Mont Blanc pen?"

He nodded grudgingly. "Okay, I do have one of those, but I'm not sentimental about it."

"What are you sentimental about, Mack?"

"Now what kind of question is that?"

"Casual," she answered. "Just something to pass the time while you grope my hips."

"I am not groping. I'm trying to get loose. But I will certainly try harder not to touch you."

Eliza sighed. The men she found attractive always seemed to be trying not to touch her. It was very frustrating. "Can I ask you something?" She felt him tense and didn't wait for an answer. "Do you think I'm attractive? I mean, not to you personally, of course, but just—"

"Yes."

"—in general." She paused. "Yes?"

"Yes."

That was it? No explanation? And he hadn't even hesitated, either. "Attractive in general, you mean."

His arm rubbed against hers. "I mean just what I said. You're attractive. Now, could you move your hand a little? I may be making progress."

She wanted to ask him if he thought the dress made the difference, but there really hadn't been much opportunity for him to admire the gown. And she certainly didn't want to sound like she was asking for reassurance...which she wasn't. She'd just wanted an opinion, and since he was the only man to see her in the Worth gown—except for Chuck, who didn't count—she'd thought he might—

"Are you still back there?"

His curt question interrupted her thoughts, and she moved her hand...probably a whole sixteenth of an inch, but she let her fingertips dust the slope of his hips in the process. Tight end, she thought, and then hastily curled her fingers into her palms. What was she doing? He was married, for heaven's sake. Well, not married, but only by a quirk of fate. And even if he'd missed the ceremony, he still belonged to another woman. The beautiful Leanne.

"How long have you known her?" Eliza hunched her shoulders to stretch the stiff muscles in her neck and back.

"Known who?"

"Your fiancée."

"Oh. Leanne. Mmm, a long time. Since she was born, I suppose."

"And how long is that?"

"What?"

Eliza hadn't thought it took such total concentration to wiggle one's hands. "How old is Leanne?"

"Mmm. Twenty-six, maybe? I'm not sure."

"You're going to marry her and you don't know how old she is? Do you remember her birthday?"

"She makes sure of it."

"You sound like you've been married for years."

"Sometimes it feels that way."

Eliza dropped her head back again and looked through the roof at the stars. "I hope I never feel that way. When I'm a hundred and eight and have been married for a thousand years, I want to be as much in love as the day I fall into it."

"Fall into what?"

She frowned. "Love, Mack. The day I fall in love. And if it requires so much effort to keep from touching me, then please grope. It's important to have a little conversation, too, I think. I mean, we've been tied together for more than a half hour. Aren't you the least bit curious about me?"

"That's a trick question if I ever heard one."

"All right, we can talk about you. Or Leanne. Or old barns. I don't care, as long as I don't have to sit here and think about Mrs. Pageatt and the wedding dress and how much trouble I'm going to be in when she finds out I don't have it anymore."

Mack cleared his throat. "Excuse the pun, but isn't that like shutting the barn door after the horse is out?"

"If you don't mind, let's not talk about horses, either."

"Why not? Did you get thrown off one once or something?"

"I'm not crazy enough to *ride* one of them." Eliza shivered slightly at the thought. "They're big and they snort and snuffle, and I've just never liked them, that's all."

He stopped fumbling with the cables. "You mean you gave away our one chance to take Chuck by surprise because you 'just never liked' horses?"

She decided she owed him at least a partial confession. "Maybe I'm a little frightened by them."

"I think I'd feel better if you admitted you were downright terrified of them."

"How can you be so sure you would have hit Chuck, anyway? You might have missed even if you'd had the element of surprise."

His fingers grazed her hip as he moved his hands again. "I am curious about one thing. Why did you steal the dress in the first place?"

"In the first and every other place, I did not *steal* the Worth gown." She scooted irritably as far away as the cables would allow, which was hardly any distance at all. "I can't believe you even asked me that."

"Considering you were wearing the damn dress, it seemed like a fair question. How would anyone know you were only borrowing it?"

"I just tried it on," she said in self-defense. "And then the sleeve button got snagged and Mrs. Pageatt came in and it started to rain and there you were in the limousine. It was all completely innocent."

He didn't say anything for a few minutes. "Does this kind of 'completely innocent' chain of events happen to you very often?"

She was suddenly sorry she'd encouraged him to talk. "Once in a while," she hedged. "Not every day."

"Good, then we have something to look forward to tomorrow."

"You know, Mack, it isn't kind to keep reminding me that if I hadn't gotten into your limo we wouldn't be tied up in this barn now. I have said I was sorry and I am. I've offered to explain everything to Leanne and I will. But in the meantime, I'd appreciate a little consideration for my feelings."

At her words, he went still...and then he twisted his wrist inside the cable knot until he could clasp her hand in his. "You're right. It isn't fair to blame you for everything. I'm sure, over the course of this long evening, I made some contribution to this melodrama."

Wrapped around hers, his hand felt warm and comforting and very nice. "You did eat my hamburger," she said.

"You didn't want it."

"I didn't then, but I sure wish I had it now."

He squeezed her fingers. "Hungry, huh?"

"Yes. You know what would be really good right now?"

"A pair of cable cutters."

"A hot dog slathered with catsup and mustard and covered with onions, relish and sauerkraut." She ran her tongue over her lips. "Oh, and a sprinkling of cheese. Not a whole lot. Just enough to add color."

"Any more 'color' on that bun and your veins would collapse in self-defense. Don't you know hot dogs are one of the worst things you can put into your body?''

"Oh, like Buddy's Burgers are high on the nutrition chart." She moved her shoulders up and down to loosen her stiff muscles. "And you had a milk shake, too."

"Guilty. On the other hand, you're starving and I'm not."

"Thanks for pointing that out. I feel better already."

He squeezed her hand and she squeezed back. "When we get out of this barn, I'll buy you a hot dog," he said. "How's that?"

"Considering Chuck took your wallet, that's a bit unrealistic."

"Right. No wallet. Well, we'll figure some way around that. Maybe we're close to a Western Union office and someone can wire us emergency cash."

"And who do you think is going to do that?"

He stopped, then stroked his thumb across the top of her hand, sending a ripple of response up her arm. "Someone will," he said vaguely. "The main thing is to get out of . . . this . . . blasted tangle."

Tangle. He wasn't offering or asking for solace with all his hand squeezing and thumb stroking. Oh, no. All he was worried about was getting their hands through the knotted cable. She jerked her hand the half inch it took to get away from his.

He grabbed it back.

"You're compulsive, Mack. Did you know that? Completely compulsive."

"I have my moments. Now would you mind turning your wrist just a little?"

"I would mind, so don't ask."

He exhaled, sighing heavily. "Do you want to be tied to me for the rest of your life?"

"Arrogant, too." She stiffened and leaned away from him. "Compulsive *and* arrogant."

"I am trying to save your life here. I don't think a little cooperation from you is too much to ask."

He was right. She was behaving like a complete imbecile, wanting to hold hands with him instead of working with him for the perfectly reasonable goal of freedom. "I'm sorry. I don't normally act like a spoiled child. What do you want me to do?"

All was quiet for a moment, as if he had to consider her request, and then he dropped his head back and looked up. "I want you to tell me again what you see up there."

Puzzled, she tossed her head back and looked at the sky. "Stars, sky, a couple of stray clouds."

"But no hole in the roof."

She frowned. "Well, sure. If there wasn't a hole, I wouldn't be able to see anything except the roof."

He threaded his fingers through hers and squeezed . . . and this time she knew he meant it. "You're a strange woman, Eliza."

"You're a little peculiar yourself, Mack."

He laughed. "Under the circumstances, I'll take that as a compliment. Are you ready to give the knot another go?"

"Ready to wiggle when you are."

"Save the wiggle for a minute and see if you can get hold of one of the clamps. If we could just get those off . . ."

"I can touch one with my right hand." She groped for the handle. "But I can't get my fingers around it."

"Okay. What happens if I move like this?" He turned one shoulder toward her.

"No, that pulls it farther away. Try the other direction."

He scooted and maneuvered, pressing hard against her side. "Now?" he asked.

"Almost."

The cable drew painfully tight across her waist as he strained into the turn. She could tell by his quickened breathing that it hurt him as well, but he held the position. "Now try," he said.

She grappled with the clamp, straining to get a solid grip. "Come on, baby," she murmured. "Come on.... Come...got it!" She squeezed hard once and then again. On the third try, the clamp came free in her hand. "I got it!"

"Good," he said, sighing. "We should have thought of this before. Grope around and see if you can get hold of another one."

She groped. "Nope, nothing. You try."

"Scoot toward me. That's right. Turn your shoulder in and... Good. I can almost... Turn a little more. A little more. More. There. Got it."

Mack smiled with relief as the clamp came loose in his hand. They weren't free by any means, but at least they were making progress. With steady pressure, he tugged at the knots and felt the cable give just a little. "Pull, Eliza. And keep turning toward me."

"I'm trying, but... It slipped." Her voice rose with excitement. "The knot slipped. I felt it." She scooted farther into the turn and her shoulder dipped behind his. "It slipped again."

"Keep going. Keep—" His breath caught the instant he felt her breast brush his arm.

"I can almost reach the other clamp," she said eagerly. "If I can turn just a little more..."

He felt the tug as she gripped the third clamp and gave it a yank. Two more tugs and it, too, was free. With another twist, she was sitting at a skewed right angle to him, and her breast was pressing into the back of his shoulder. Like a thief caught in the act, awareness ran for cover all across his body.

"Mack?"

Her soft query snapped him from the moment of fantasy to the problem at hand. "I've almost got the last one," he said as he belatedly fished for the remaining terminal clamp. In another moment he had it, and in the next, it dangled loose.

"You did it!" She laughed with relief. "Now, if I shake my hand like this—" she wiggled her hand, and her breast rubbed up and down against him "—and if you'll just move your hand like that..."

He hardly noticed when the cable slid across his wrist.

"I'm out!" She pulled one hand free and shook it vigorously. "Boy, does it tingle, too. How are you doing with yours?"

His was preoccupied with the tantalizing touch of her breast against his skin, and the tingling he felt at the moment was highly inappropriate. Eliza's movements were completely innocent, he knew. Even with one hand free, she was still bound to him at the waist, and there simply wasn't any other position available to her. But he had absolutely no business noticing how soft, full and delightfully contoured she was. And his body had even less business responding to that information.

Frustrated, he jerked futilely against the loop at his wrist, again and again.

"Slow down," she said. "Take your time and twist your hand, easy-like."

He closed his eyes, took a deep, focusing breath and concentrated on the back-and-forth, twisting movement of his hand. The cable scraped over his knuckles, fell away, and the whole system of loops and knots went slack. Extricating his other hand was relatively easy after that. In tandem with Eliza, he worked the knots, pulling and pushing the clamps through the loops, passing the cable ends to her and taking them back again as they unraveled the confining bonds.

"Hooray!" Eliza jumped up and did a little war dance, stomping her feet and waving her arms, apparently oblivious to the dilemma that now faced them.

Keeping his back to her, Mack pushed himself to his feet and focused his energy on the achy, throbbing awakening of his stiff muscles as he tried mightily to ignore the inclination—no, make that persistent impulse—to turn around and take a good, long look at her, which was all too possible with the brightness of the moonlight streaming through a hold in the roof.

"Mack?"

He cleared his throat and looked steadfastly at the barn wall. "Yes?"

"Do you see a horse blanket anywhere on your side of the barn?"

"A horse blanket?"

"Or a fig leaf. You know. Anything I might be able to cover up with."

A rush of empathy for all the indignities she had suffered this evening rose above his own self-consciousness. "Sorry," he said in an intentionally light, conversational tone. "Nothing over here but a handful of moldy hay."

Her sigh was audible and forlorn. "Same here. A whole barn full of nothing."

"You'd think Tamra and Jake would have left a quilt or a blanket lying around, wouldn't you?" he said to ease the tension.

"Jake keeps it in his truck."

"His truck." He nodded as if they were talking about real people. "That makes sense, I guess."

"Well, yes, it does. Especially when you realize that she drives a hatchback."

He smiled, wondering if it was the stress that brought out this imaginative streak in her. "Just as a matter of interest, is it a quilt or a blanket?"

"It's a red-checked tablecloth. Fabric, not plastic coated."

He acknowledged that bit of information with a nod he knew she wouldn't see, and continued to stare at the shabby barn wall as he stretched his stiff muscles. A minute ticked past and then another. She coughed. He cleared his throat and did a couple of side-to-side twists, which gave him an intriguing, sideways glimpse of moonlit skin and supple curves.

Not that he was looking, although he wanted to. But he wouldn't, of course. Or if he did, it would be just a casual look. Maybe a glance while they discussed how to handle...no, no *handling*. They would discuss how to get help just as they would if they were wearing clothes. Being naked was immaterial, completely irrelevant.

"I should probably step outside and take a look around," he said.

"I'll come with you," she said immediately. "We need to stay together."

"No. No, we don't." His response was every bit as quick on the trigger as hers had been. "You'll be safer staying inside the barn." From the corner of his eye, he saw her turn her head and look at him over her shoulder.

"Safer than what?"

"Than wandering around outside."

"But you'll be wandering around out there, Mack. And I'll be with you."

He rubbed his thumb across his jaw. "Eliza, a naked man wandering around will attract less attention than a naked woman. Or a naked couple."

"Oh."

"So you can see why you need to stay in here while I go for help."

"I can see that we're going to have to get past being naked, that's for sure. So let's just turn around and get it over with."

Her suggestion tossed his thoughts like a Caesar salad. "Get what over with?" he asked cautiously.

"Being self-conscious about not having any clothes on. We can't keep standing here with our backs turned, pretending we're not aware of each other. Well, maybe you can. But I can't. And we're never going to figure out a plan of action if we have to keep talking to the walls."

He straightened his shoulders. "I'm trying to preserve some dignity for you, Eliza."

"That's sweet, Mack, especially since this is all my fault. But I'm turning around...and I suggest you do likewise."

Amazing, he thought. He had actually believed this clumsy situation couldn't get any worse.

Chapter Six

"There, now," Eliza said with conspicuous bravado as they faced each other across a few feet of barn floor. "This isn't so bad, is it?"

No. *Bad* was not a word Mack would use to describe what he was feeling at the moment. *Admiring* came to mind. *Awake,* too...his whole body was now definitely awake—and aroused. Unfortunately, there was that, too. Draping his hands casually over the rising evidence, he began silently reciting every phone number he had ever memorized.

"See? All we needed was to get over the initial shock." Eliza chattered on, as if a naked stranger crossed her line of vision at least once a day. He noted, however, in a mental pause between counting off the numbers of his office phone and his cellular, that she kept her gaze pinned somewhere near his right ear. "So now," she continued, "we're past the self-consciousness phase and we can get on with...well, with whatever comes next."

"Getting out of here," he suggested in the same edgy tone. "We should get out of here."

"Right. There's probably a farmhouse nearby. That makes sense, don't you think? I mean, if there's a barn here, there's bound to be a farmer somewhere in the area.''

Mack reached Leanne's number on his phone list and his mind went blank. Frowning, he tried to remember it...and failed completely. Not even the first digit surfaced in his thoughts. Another effect of the day's stress, he supposed. At least he was feeling more in control of his body, even if his life had taken a startling detour.

Not that any change in his plans wouldn't have been startling, but being kidnapped from the jaws of matrimony had thrown him into a particularly strange state of mind. He felt...well, *free,* for lack of a better word. Free. And very fortunate, as if he'd just been handed a reprieve. That feeling could be nothing more than simple relief that he was here and not face-to-face with his fiancée, attempting to explain the odd sequence of events that had led to his missing the wedding she had planned to perfection.

Of course, Leanne would eventually understand that he had had no choice in the matter. But right now, amidst the rubble of the wedding that hadn't come off, she would not be in a reasonable or forgiving mood. In fact, he figured that by this time she had cut out his face from every one of her photographs in which he had the audacity to appear. To show her support, Mother Bankston probably had had him blackballed from the country club. His own mother, too, would still be thinking the worst. And his grandfather...well, Grandfather never knew what was going on anyway. As Eliza had so aptly put it, this had not been a banner day.

But Mack was in good spirits. Better spirits, actually, than he'd been in before Eliza had crash-landed in the limousine. Of course, his high spirits could be attributed to any number of things. Surviving a kidnapping was one. Having no bullet holes anywhere in his body was another. Even the fact that he'd been stripped naked in a barn had its humorous side. He doubted he would ever admit that to anyone, except maybe Eliza. She had a sense of humor. And courage. She had that, too.

Wait a minute. He looked around the shadowed barn. Where was she? A few seconds ago she'd been standing right in front of him, chattering nervously, pretending she didn't mind the awful awkwardness of their situation, keeping her chin high, as if she wasn't just as embarrassed as he. Now where could she have gone? "Hello?" he said tentatively. "Eliza?"

A cricket chirped in reply. It was clear she was no longer in the barn, so she must have walked outside while he was concentrating on phone numbers and the mood back home.

"Eliza?" he called more forcefully as he moved to the doorway. The moon bathed the countryside in a shaded glow, spreading enough light to reveal that she was not in the immediate vicinity.

A fearful dread struck his heart dead center. What had happened to her? How could she have disappeared so fast? Had Chuck returned and nabbed her the moment she'd left the barn? Had she hurt herself somehow? Where in the hell was she?

"Eliza!" he snapped, and the cricket stopped chirping.

She walked around the near corner of the barn as if taking a stroll in her birthday suit was nothing out of the ordinary. Her head tilted back, she was looking up at the sky, stargazing with the curious expression of a child contemplating the universe. The moonlight cast a soft, luminous glow over her skin, shading the contours of her full breasts, trim waist and long legs, revealing her natural beauty as an artist might in painting her portrait. He swallowed hard and focused his energy on an assumed annoyance rather than a very real attraction. "Eliza," he said irritably.

At the sound of his voice, she stopped and looked at him with surprise. "Mack. Hi. Were you looking for me?"

"You shouldn't wander off by yourself." His tone was gruff, overly intense, and he cleared his throat to soothe it. "It could be dangerous out here."

"I don't see how. It's so quiet. Did you notice? And the stars are so close, I think if I were a little taller, I could grab a whole handful of them."

Her smile was bright and beguiling, but he refused to give in to it. "Where were you?"

Her smile vanished. "I came outside for a little privacy. You seemed lost in thought and I figured you could use a few minutes by yourself, too."

"You could have told me you were leaving."

Her chin rose. "You could have watched me walk out of the barn, if you hadn't been so busy staring at the wall."

"I was being courteous and considerate of your feelings."

"Yes, Mack, I know. And I appreciate what a gentleman you've been throughout this whole thing. But I like to look at a person when I'm talking to him and I like for people to look at me when they're talking to me. And when you look *past* me instead of *at* me, it only reminds me of the reason you *can't* look at me and—and I wish you'd just stop it."

He wished he'd stop it, too. What did he find so all-fired appealing about this voluptuous little sprite? Considering all the trouble she'd caused, he shouldn't have the remotest desire to put his hands anywhere on her, except maybe around her neck. But her neck was slender and pretty, and a man could trail his hand right down...

Catching his gaze before it dropped any lower, he made another effort to recall Leanne's phone number.

"See? You're doing it again," Eliza said, sighing. "Can't you just pretend we're visiting a nudist colony?"

What a ridiculous thought that was. "Sorry, but that is beyond my powers of imagination."

She tipped her head to the side and frowned at him. "You're lost without a pocket to put your planner in, aren't you, Mack? Look, will it help if I say that I have no designs on your virtue or your body? Not that it isn't a great body, you understand. I mean, I'd be lying if I said I didn't look. But I can't even remember the last time I seduced a man. I've completely forgotten how. Even if I knew how, I have a strict rule about seducing married men... and if we hadn't gotten kidnapped, you would be married, so you can see that you're completely safe with me. And when this is all over, I will happily explain to Leanne how you behaved like a perfect gentleman."

"I'm planning to leave out this part of the story."

"Really?" Her forehead furrowed, showing her confusion. "I don't see why you would. Knowing you're a gentleman out of your clothes as well as in them will only strengthen the respect she has for you."

"Mmm-hmm," he said, knowing exactly what kind of respect Leanne would give any such explanation... if he was idiot enough to offer it. Or worse, if Eliza tried to do so. "Let's just concentrate our energy on getting home safely, shall we?"

"Oh, Mack, I forgot!" Her eyes widened with excitement. "You're never going to believe what I found. I was coming to tell you when you walked out. Come over here. You have to see this."

He started forward, thinking rescue was just around the corner, wondering how she could have forgotten to tell him immediately. "A house?" he guessed. "A car? Clothes?"

"A haystack."

He stopped walking. "A haystack?"

"Yes. Can you believe it? Not a bale of hay anywhere in the barn, but there's a whole haystack right out there in the field. I've never seen one, except in movies. With the moon shining on it, it looks like a big, gold thimble."

"A haystack," he repeated.

She pursed her lips. "Oh, come on, Mack. There's no need to act so incredulous. I just want you to see it."

"Eliza, we've been kidnapped, stripped and left in the middle of nowhere. At this moment, I'd be glad to see almost anything *except* a haystack. Now, I am going for help and I don't want to have to worry about you getting snared up in a barbed-wire fence while I'm gone. So, please, go back inside the barn and wait for me."

"A snowman," she said, confidently nodding. "I bet you wouldn't be glad to see one of those at this moment."

He stared at her, wondering how she could be lost, naked and cheerful all at the same time. "You're right. If I had to choose between a snowman and a haystack, the hay would win hands down. Now, will you go back inside the barn?"

She balanced on one foot and rubbed the back of her calf with her toes. "No, I don't think so."

"Oh, come on, Eliza. You can't go wandering all over the countryside. Not... like that."

"Like what?"

He recognized the flash of contrariness in the faint lift of her chin. "You cannot wander around out here without any clothes on."

"Why not? You are."

"*I* am going for help."

"And *I* am going to get a closer look at the haystack." She took a step backward while offering him a persuasive smile. "Who knows when I'll ever be in western Kansas again? And it's a nice, warm night. The moon is out. And since we have to cut across the field to go for help anyway, we can stop to look at the haystack on our way."

Her logic exhausted him. "The road is in that direction." He pointed the other way. "And that silly haystack is not on *our* way anywhere. Now, here's how this is going to work. You will stay in the barn. I will go for help. Period. End of discussion."

"End of discussion," she repeated with a definitive nod...just before she turned and disappeared around the corner of the barn, leaving him in the shadows, feeling like he'd been sideswiped by a John Deere tractor.

"Eliza!"

Silence. He tried again, louder and more insistently. "Eliza!"

A second passed, and another, before her head popped around the corner. "Yo!"

"Would you come back here?"

"Is the discussion reopened?"

"No. But I can't go for help until you're safe inside the barn."

"How do you know I won't be safer *outside* the barn?"

He tamped down his irritation. "Please go inside and wait for me."

She lifted her one visible shoulder in a shrug. "Can't. Sorry." Her voice expressed her regret. "I just can't be this close to the only haystack I've ever laid eyes on and not go and look for the proverbial needle."

"Eliza!" But she was gone again. Damn. No wonder they were in this predicament. The woman had no focus. No ability to make a plan and stick to it. He would have thought she'd be anxious to stay inside the barn where she'd be safe and reasonably comfortable while he braved the perils of a strange countryside. But, no. She went running off to see a pile of straw. In the middle of the night. In her bare feet. In the buff.

That thought produced a provocative image of Eliza running through a freshly mown field, her dark hair bouncing in the moonlight, her body moving in sensuous slow motion. And in his mind's eye, he watched her approach, admiring her beauty, smiling as she neared, opening his arms to take her in, falling back into a nest of hay....

He slapped at a mosquito. He must be out of his mind. She had brought more mischief into his life in the last several hours than he'd experienced in all of the preceding years. He was going to marry Leanne. If not for Eliza, he'd already be married. So why was he walking purposefully around the corner of the barn, heading toward the field like some moonstruck Romeo?

Concern for her safety, he told himself...and wished he believed it.

SHE WAS MAKING A MESS of an already messy situation.

Eliza reached the haystack and that conclusion at the same time and didn't like either one. The haystack had appeared romantic from a distance, a touch of nostalgia plunked into a night of misadventures. Just like her feeble idea that if she could get Mack to look at the haystack, he magically would forget all the havoc she'd caused tonight.

Wrinkling her nose, she inhaled the musty scent of the hay, then reached out to touch it. A single piece poked into her palm and promptly broke in half. Fragile stuff, she thought. It was a wonder it could be stacked like this. She gave it a push with the butt of her hand. Sturdy, too. Stepping back, she looked up at the rounded top, a foot or more above her head. She'd seen movies that showed people hiding on top of haystacks. She could even remember one movie in which a couple made love up there.

Of course, that was Hollywood in its *hay*-day. Smiling at her pun, she moved closer and tested the sturdiness of the stack with a second, stronger punch. A few straws snapped beneath the pressure, but that was it. She was impressed. She knew that haystacks were mostly a thing of the past, relics of an era when

harvesting a field depended more on muscle power
than on machines. Modern hay balers were undoubtedly more efficient, but a dozen precision-tied bun-
dles would never have the appeal of one honest-to-
goodness haystack.

It made her proud to know that at least one Kansas
farmer still knew how to stack his hay. She took her
hat off to whoever had built this straw bulwark. That
is, if she had a hat to take off in tribute, she would.
Instead, she bumped the haystack with a simultaneous one-two jab of her shoulder and hip, like a foot-
ball player congratulating a fellow team member on a
great play.

"What in the hell are you doing?" a deep voice
blared into the quiet, scaring her out of her wits. With
a high-pitched shriek, she dove for cover...and the
whole, stalwart haystack crumbled on top of her.

"GOOD GRIEF, Eliza, you could have suffocated under there."

She raked her teeth across her tongue and spit out a
piece of hay. "If you hadn't snuck up on me, I
wouldn't have been under there."

Mack fell back against the hay, put his hands behind his head and stared up at the stars. "If I had a
lick of sense, I'd be a mile away from here by now."

"Trying to hitch a ride on a deserted road." She
dropped back onto the hay beside him. "In my opinion, hitchhiking represents less than half a lick of
sense. You could get picked up by some evil, twisted
person. Or you could be abducted by space aliens."

"I wish you'd told me I had other options," he said.
"I thought renting a limousine and getting kid-

napped by an evil, twisted person was my only choice."

"Very funny. And just for the record, I don't believe Chuck is evil or twisted." Eliza shifted on the straw bed, trying to get comfortable. "He's a liar...that goes without saying. And a thief. That goes without saying, too. But he didn't shoot us. And he did buy a round of Buddy's Burgers. Of course, you ate mine. But all things considered, I think he treated us pretty decently."

The hay rustled as Mack turned his head to look at her. "Would that 'all things considered' include the bullet that missed my foot by a half inch? Or the half hour or more we spent tied up in jumper cables? Or would that just include the demoniac laugh he gave as he walked out of the barn with our clothes?"

He had a point. "All right," she conceded. "So it would have been more fun to be abducted by aliens."

"At least we could have sold an abduction story to the tabloids."

"You can sell the kidnapping story, if you want. I hereby relinquish my rights."

"Thank you, I accept . . . considering that I did risk my sensitive skin to save you just now."

"That makes twice in one day you've saved me." She scratched her elbow. "I hope you don't expect me to be indebted to you for the rest of my life, though. I wouldn't be very good at following you around, waiting for an opportunity to save your life and repay my debt."

"You don't owe me anything, Eliza, no matter how many times I save you."

She yawned, feeling warm and sheltered, if a bit itchy, in her pocket of hay. "Well, what if all of a sudden a big herd of cows stampedes through this field and you have to throw yourself in front of the biggest one and scare it away so the rest of the herd will swerve to miss me? And what if the big cow steps on your foot and breaks your toe? What about that?"

"In case of stampede, no debt."

"No compensation for the broken toe?"

"Just one of the hazards of being a hero. I should have been more careful."

"Hmm." She stared at the brilliant sky and absently scratched her stomach. "Well, what if some big, black clouds roll in and all of a sudden a tornado swoops out of the sky and whirls us away to Idaho or some strange place?"

"Oz or Idaho. I'll see that you're returned to Kansas."

She would have frowned at him, but it didn't seem worth the trouble of turning her head. "All right, MacKenzie, what exactly do you expect to get out of this bargain?"

"Peace of mind."

Raising herself on her elbow, she picked up a fistful of hay and dropped it on his face. "I'll bet you say that to all the girls."

In one neat toss, he clobbered her with straw. She sputtered under the onslaught . . . and retaliated with a blind pitch. A moment later, she was inundated with flying fodder and the agreeable sound of laughter . . . her own and Mack's. Scrambling for advantage in the slippery hay, she managed to smash a handful of straw into his hair before he grabbed her wrist and wrestled her down.

"Didn't your mother ever tell you to pick fights with somebody your own size?" he asked.

Using her foot as a pitchfork, she deluged him. "What my Auntie Gem told me," she said between gasps of laughter, "was that men...are poor...losers."

He bowed his head against the smothering shower...and she caught a mouthful of straw and sucked it in on a snort of laughter. She choked, coughed and wheezed in the effort to catch her breath.

Mack grabbed her arm, jerked her upright and whopped her between the shoulder blades with the heel of his hand. "Spit it out," he said fiercely, thumping her back between instructions. "Don't swallow. Get it out of your mouth. Cough. Come on, spit it out."

She coughed. And spit. And coughed some more.

Mack gave her another whack on the back and she all but toppled off the collapsed haystack. As she wheezed a great gulp of air into her lungs, she grabbed his hand and yanked it away from her back. "That is not...the way—" she gulped more air "—to do the...Heimlich...maneuver."

"Well, excuse me. Next time you're choking, I'll ask for instructions." With a shaky sigh, he put his head back and closed his eyes. "At least I wasn't trying to give you mouth-to-mouth."

She swiped her hand across her lips, trying to get rid of the dry, dusty taste, trying not to imagine what would have happened if he'd put his lips on hers for any reason. "Do you even know how?"

"How to what?"

"To resuscitate someone."

"Yes, I know *how*." He turned his head and frowned at her. "Why? Are you planning to dive into a cow pond and try to drown?"

She frowned right back at him. "I was asking because I just finished taking a CPR course and I thought that if you didn't know, I'd explain how it's done."

"Right. Like we need to practice mouth-to-mouth resuscitation out here in this haystack."

"I didn't say anything about practicing."

"No, you didn't." He leaned forward and rested his arms on his raised knees. "That thought was all my own."

A shiver loped down her spine, shifting her focus, until all she could do was sit there and admire his muscular back and shoulders. His dark hair reflected a glint of silver, and his skin held the sheen of moonlit gold. The urge to touch him was compelling, but she resolutely curled her fingers into the straw. "Well, it was a nice thought."

He turned his head. Their eyes met and held...and awareness wove into the very air she was still trying so hard to breathe.

"Yes," he said finally. "A nice thought, but not a good idea."

She nodded hastily. "Oh, right. You're absolutely right. I hope you know I wasn't suggesting we should..." A slightly panicked laugh escaped her. "Well, people can't just go around practicing mouth-to-mouth, now can they? I mean, you and I know that CPR is very serious..." Her bravado deserted her and she ended with a murmured, "...stuff."

He turned away, restoring her view of the back of his head. "We weren't talking about CPR, Eliza."

A second shiver rolled down her back. "We weren't?"

"No."

"Oh." She knew that was the end of the discussion, but her mouth was too quick for her own good. "So if we weren't talking about mouth-to-mouth resuscitation, we must have been talking about one of those you-can't-think-of-any-other-way-to-shut-me-up kisses. Right?"

"That would be one way of putting it," he confirmed, his voice distant, but edgy.

"I always have talked too much." She sighed. "Auntie Gem says that my nerves are miswired to my mouth somehow, and when I get nervous, everything goes haywire and it takes an act of God to shut me up. Not that I'm comparing your kisses to an act of God, you understand, but... well, I mean, how would *I* know? You didn't *really* kiss me. Twice. It was just a kind of self-defense both times. At least, that's what I thought."

His silent stillness unnerved her even more. "You don't have to worry, Mack. I wouldn't misinterpret something like that. I know you're in love with Leanne, and if Chuck hadn't waylaid you, you'd be married and off on your honeymoon instead of here with me. You don't have to give it another thought. I understand perfectly."

Tension knotted his shoulders. "I'm glad *you* do. Because at this moment all I understand is that I am not married, I am here with you and, if you don't stop talking, I am going to kiss you."

She gulped as a new awareness paralyzed her vocal cords and bathed her in revealing insight. She was alone with a man who attracted her in ways no other man ever had. In a few hours, they had shared a range of emotions that now bound them in a tenuous and tenacious coalition. Their destinies had collided in the rain-wet parking lot of the Marry We Go Bridal Boutique, and the resulting whirlwind of complications had dropped them, naked, into a dust-dry hayfield in western Kansas.

Now that she thought about it, being naked probably had a lot to do with the tension she was feeling right now. And it probably had everything to do with the reason Mack wanted to kiss her. It was simple. Men and women were sexual beings. She was a woman, Mack was a man and they were naked in a haystack in the moonlight. Logic all but dictated they would be aware of each other. Human nature practically decreed that a kiss, more or less, would cross their minds.

She sighed and plopped back in the hay. "I really hate simple explanations."

"If there is one thing simple about what is happening here, I'd like to know what it is."

She shouldn't answer, shouldn't say a word. Should not open her... "Lust," she said. "It's that simple. Here we are, all alone. It's night. We're naked. Lust was bound to crop up...so to speak."

She was conscious of his movement as he turned. She was conscious of the silent debate he waged as his gaze slid across her belly, her breasts, and traveled on to her mouth. She was conscious of the invitation she issued with the slight parting of her lips.

"You talk too much, Eliza," Mark said decisively. His hand came to rest beside her shoulder, and on some level of awareness, she knew he was sliding down into the nest of hay beside her. But she couldn't drag her attention from the swirl of lusty anticipation inside her any more than she could drag her gaze from the slow descent of his mouth.

"Mack," she whispered in a dying effort to halt fate in its tracks. "I'm not insured against acts of God."

"Shut up, Eliza."

Chapter Seven

Shut up, Eliza....

His lips sealed the command, closing over hers with a sweetness born of sublime astonishment. He hadn't intended to kiss her. Hell, he had *intended* to be halfway to somewhere else by now...somewhere he could ask for and receive assistance, somewhere with telephone service, somewhere Eliza wasn't. But here he was, in a haystack, under the spell of a waning moon, kissing her with purpose and the enthusiastic support of his body.

Lust. Well, she was right about that, anyway. He couldn't remember the last time he'd wanted to kiss a woman until she melted with desire. But he wanted Eliza to forget that she had ever been kissed before. From this minute on, he wanted her to think of him whenever she saw a starlit sky. He wanted her to forever associate the musty-sweet smell of hay with the feel of his hand on her bare skin. He wanted her to recall the taste of his lips every time any other man touched her. He wanted any kisses she received in the future to be tainted with the memory of this one, wicked, lustful kiss.

He hoped that was simple enough for her.

He rolled onto his side, pulling her with him into the coarse, warm nest of hay. With a few deft touches, he aligned her against him and gathered her close in his arms. She came to him easily, provocatively, like a woman who knew what she wanted. Yet her hands curled lightly against his chest, as if she had no idea where to put them. The soft purling in her throat was a siren's song of pure pleasure, but she shyly held her body away from intimacy, receptive to the pressure of his hand, but taking no initiative of her own.

Deepening the kiss, he circled her wrist with his fingers and brought her arm up around his neck. She seemed to like that idea and began to stroke his hair and neck without further encouragement. Her breasts, firm and aroused, brushed his chest with tantalizing timidity. He trailed his hand down her spine, knowing from experience how long to linger in any one spot, caressing her, then moving on, moving lower, relaxing her with a fleeting massage. And still, despite the sensual coaxing of her lips under his, despite the delightful, teasing response of her tongue to his advance, her inexperience was obvious and surprising. Maybe she'd been telling the truth when she'd said she didn't remember how to seduce a man.

He tightened the pressure of his mouth on hers and wished he could claim she *had* tried to seduce him. But the responsibility for this misguided kiss of exploration and discovery was entirely his. She was innocent of everything except assuring him that he was safe with her... and of bringing lust into the equation. She wasn't exactly innocent there.

Still, he had no right to kiss her, not like this. Not like he meant it. Not like he'd been waiting all of his life for this moment, this kiss... and her.

She pulled away suddenly, before he had quite decided the moment should end.

"What was that?" she whispered.

He found her wide-eyed surprise naively appealing. "I believe you called it lust."

"Not that. *That.*"

"That?"

"Yes, that." She lay very still and stared into his eyes. "There. Do you feel that?"

He felt aroused—and erect. And ashamed of himself for letting the situation get this far out of hand. "Eliza, *that* is the normal male reaction to..." His explanation foundered and sank like a rock as her eyes widened further with shock.

"Normal?" She breathed the word out in panic. "That can't be nor*mal!*"

The last syllable came out in a shriek as she jerked her knee up, hitting him in the groin and clobbering every amorous thought he had ever entertained. Every muscle in his body clenched in protest against the pain that shot through him with the speed of light. With his eyes closed in agony, he rolled onto his back and let a deep, heartfelt groan ooze from his throat.

He was dimly conscious of her jerky movements and of her scramble to get her feet up and away from the edge of the slippery hay. And he was vaguely aware that she was talking to someone or something. But he was in no condition to care what she was doing or why. At least, not until her panicked whisper penetrated his anguish.

"Mack, do something."

Strangling her seemed appropriate, but he didn't have the strength. At the moment, he didn't have the strength even to answer her.

Her next sound was a startled, indrawn breath. "Go away. Shoo! Don't come any closer. Shoo!" Her hand fanned the air over his stomach. "Shoo! Mack, quick, we need a silver bullet."

By squinting and partially lifting his head, he managed to decipher the secret code. "Silver bullet" equaled werewolf, equaled a big, fuzzy dog sniffing along the perimeter of the haystack. Its plumed tail was wagging, and the animal looked domestic and friendly. Mack dropped back on the hay, moistened his lips and managed to mutter, "Don't...shoot. He's...unarmed."

"Oh, sure. You say that now, but wait until he sinks his fangs into your ankle."

Mack struggled to sit up while still coiled in a protective position. "Did he...bite...you?"

"Shoo! Get out of here." She waved the dog away. "He *licked* me."

With a hefty and exasperated groan, Mack crumpled into the hay one more time.

Her attention switched to him. "What's wrong? Did he lick you, too?"

Recuperating in silence was obviously not in the cards. "No," he said. "You...hit me."

"I did not. I heard this snuffing sound. And then I felt something warm and wet on my feet and the next thing I knew my toes were all sticky and yucky and cold and...well, I got out of the way as fast as I could. But I did not hit you. At least, not on purpose. Where does it hurt?"

The answer seemed to occur to her without his spelling it out because she answered her own question with a rush of concern. "Oh, I'm sorry! I'm *so* sorry. I didn't mean to... It was an accident. Are you going to be all right? Oh, geez, I didn't even realize I... The dog scared me and... Oh, geez. Are you sure you're all right? I mean, your voice sounds okay. Not too high-pitched or anything, but... Would it help if I—"

He sensed her reaching out to him. "*Don't*...touch me."

"Oh." She withdrew as if he were a cobra coming out of a basket. "Oh, no. No, I won't. Don't worry." She was quiet for one, possibly one and a half seconds. "If there's anything I can do, anything at all, just tell me, okay? Do you need to stand up? Walk around a little? Stretch your muscles?"

"I just need to lie here."

"Fine. Okay. I'll be right here. Right beside you. In case you need help... or anything."

If he had gone for help as he'd intended to do, none of this would have happened. He wouldn't be lying in a dusty, scratchy, crumbly mound of hay wondering if he would ever be able to sire children, talk in his normal baritone or even walk again.

"Mack?" Her voice was a soft nudge, as if she thought he might be asleep. "Mack?"

He opened his eyes and looked up at her conciliatory smile.

"The dog is leaving."

"That's a relief."

She took back the smile. "I thought you'd want to know, that's all."

Compressing the ache in his body into a manageable zone of discomfort, he levered himself into a sitting position. "In the interest of my future health and well-being, I need to know if you are frightened of all four-legged animals or only select groups."

"I don't like to be licked," she said snippily. "And don't even try to pretend that you wouldn't have been startled if that dog had suddenly started licking your toes."

"You're right. I would have been, but there's an obvious difference here. You see, I *like* to be licked."

Her gaze swung to his and just as quickly swung away. "I'll bet if it had been Leanne's toes that got licked, you wouldn't find this very funny."

"True statement. But then, Leanne is handicapped."

Eliza's gaze swung back again, this time filled with concern. "She is?"

He nodded. "She was born without a funny bone."

"If you can make bad jokes, you must be feeling better."

He was, actually. Much better. And it seemed to have less to do with the receding discomfort in his body than with the fact that he was in a haystack in western Kansas instead of on his way to a honeymoon in the Bahamas. "If you knew Leanne, you'd know it's no joke."

"Of course it is," Eliza said with confidence. "You wouldn't be in love with her if she didn't have at least as good a sense of humor as yours."

"How do you know I have a sense of humor?"

"In this situation? Don't be ridiculous. The fact that you haven't murdered me speaks to that."

"Thank you," he said humbly. "I wasn't sure you'd noticed."

"Oh, please. I am fully aware it is my fault you're in this itchy old haystack and not on your way to a honeymoon in some nice, sunny, nonallergenic place like Hawaii."

"The Bahamas," he corrected absently, wondering if he really was glad to be here rather than there or just too tired to care where he was at the moment. "Leanne hates to fly."

Her questioning gaze slid toward him again. "Another joke, right?"

"No. We were scheduled to travel by train to Miami and take a cruise ship from there."

"A honeymoon on a train?" She thumped him on the arm. "And you said she has no sense of humor."

He smiled, thinking it did sound funny the way Eliza put it. But then she didn't know just how seriously Leanne took her own comfort. "Planning the honeymoon was no laughing matter."

"Well, weddings are stressful. I'm sure you found plenty of other things to laugh about."

"Oh, yeah." The memory of just how few times he'd laughed at anything during the past few months came to mind with sour solemnity. "This engagement has been a barrel of laughs."

She shook her head sadly. "Don't worry, Mack. It happens all the time."

"Unfunny engagements? Or bridegrooms being rescued at the church door?"

"Couples putting so much effort into planning the wedding, that they forget to tend to each other. Once the ceremony is over, they relax and remember why they wanted to get married in the first place. And you meant 'kidnapped.'"

"What?"

"You said 'rescued,' but you meant to say 'kidnapped at the church door.'"

"Rescued" had a nice ring to it, he thought. But then, this had been a long and confusing day. "I'm sure you're right."

"I am. Weddings are my business and I've seen this happen dozens of times." Softly yawning, she lay back against the hay and put her hands behind her head. "That's why when I have my own bridal shop, in addition to designing gowns, I'll offer a wedding-coordinating service so couples can choose to let somebody else deal with the stress while they just enjoy the special joys of their engagement."

"Obviously, you've never been engaged." He turned his head to see if she actually believed what she'd just said. But his skepticism vanished into the trail of moonbeams that sliced across her and divided her into angles of shadow and light. The path began in her silken, tousled hair and traveled across one narrow shoulder and pale, rounded breast, to the shadowed plane of her stomach and down the length of one long and shapely leg. His fingers curled into the haystack, seeking something to hold on to, anything to keep from reaching out and touching her.

"I haven't been engaged," she said. "But I know it will be a wonderful time in my life. And the wedding will be everything I've always imagined it would be. And the honeymoon will be—"

"Somewhere trains don't go."

"Heaven."

"I think you're safe. Last time I checked, heaven wasn't on the schedule."

Her laugh was a velvety rumble in her throat. "Anywhere will be heaven. Even a haystack in western Kansas will be all right with me, as long as he is there."

"He? Do you have a particular 'he' in mind?"

She patted back a yawn with her fingertips. "Yes, but he could be almost anyone."

"So this happy engagement and perfect wedding and haystack honeymoon are all a bunch of romantic folderol built around some imaginary bridegroom." He shook his head. "Well, I believe I'm speaking for an overwhelming majority of males when I say that no self-respecting bridegroom wants to spend his honeymoon sneezing and scratching in a haystack."

"You haven't sneezed once."

"But I expect to have one heck of a skin rash tomorrow." He paused. "And we were talking about your fantasy man, not me."

"Well, he won't be allergic, either." Her voice was soft, dreamy. "And since this is my fantasy, I will tell you that he is the perfect bridegroom, my best friend and my hero all rolled into one."

It was suddenly easier not to touch her. "Illusions like that are what get women into trouble. The man you're waiting for doesn't exist."

Her lips curved with the same soft, dreamy quality he'd heard in her voice. "I saw him once. Today, in fact."

"Today?" He had a half-formed, fleeting—and flattering—idea that she meant him. "Where did you meet this paragon of manhood?"

"Oh, I didn't meet him. I just saw him. In the mirror. And it could have been yesterday. I can't remember."

"You saw the man of your dreams in a mirror," he repeated. "Was he wearing a turban and did he tell you that Snow White was the fairest in the land?"

"Wrong fairy tale," she said. "He didn't say anything, and he was wearing a tuxedo. Kind of like yours, come to think of it." She yawned again and covered her mouth with the back of her hand. "He might even have licked a little like you."

Mack leaned closer, noting the droopy tilt of her eyelids. "Stay away from him, then. A *little licker* can be a dangerous thing."

"Hmm?" Her eyelids fluttered. "Don't worry. I didn't really see his face. And it was the dress, anyway." She closed her eyes for a moment, then blinked them open again. "I have to get the dress back. You do understand, don't you, Mack?"

"Of course. It's a million-dollar dress."

She offered a sweet, sleepy smile. "You're a nice person, MacKenzie. I wish you weren't already married."

He opened his mouth to dispute her statement, but she cut him off with a deep sigh and rolled away from him onto her side, curling into an enticing S. Fighting the desire to trace that alluring bare shoulder and hip with the palm of his hand, Mack leaned over her and realized that, like an exhausted child, she had simply closed her eyes and gone instantly to sleep. With her hand tucked under her cheek, she looked blissfully innocent and recklessly beautiful. Her hair fanned across her shoulder like a shadow and her eyelashes formed a crescent smudge against her cheek. Her lips were slightly parted, and he could measure the depth of her breathing by the rise and fall of moonlight on the curve of her breast. A treasure chest of tenderness spilled unexpectedly inside him, squeezing into the empty spaces around his heart.

"I'm not married, Eliza," he whispered. "You rescued me."

"Mmm." Like a mantra, her answer blended into a throaty sigh and became an unintelligible, contented murmur.

It was hard to imagine that a mere twenty-four hours ago he hadn't known her. In fact, twenty-four hours ago he had been standing on the terrace outside his bedroom, under a moon barely a sliver different from tonight's, contemplating an illicit trip out of the country. It gave him a chill now to remember the icy fingers of self-doubt and the desperate impulse to run before it was too late, before he deeded the rest of his life to Leanne in marriage.

But because he was a Cortland, he had reasoned away the doubts and wrapped the impulse in a mantle of calm reassurances. Leanne would be a perfect wife. She'd been training for the part for years. She knew the right things to say and the right times to say them. She was a gifted hostess, a dynamo of focused energy who could move between managing the kitchen and entertaining the guests without missing a name or a detail. She worked tirelessly for whatever politically correct cause caught her interest. She was a solid-gold asset in his work on behalf of the Cortland Foundation. Leanne was everything he needed in a wife.

Except a friend.

"Shoo." Eliza's forehead furrowed in a frown and she pulled her feet nearer the curve of her hips. "Don't lick me." She mumbled a few more unintelligible admonitions before her frown smoothed out and she lay still, quiet and fast asleep in the hay.

Mack bent his head to deliver a light, but rebellious lick across her shoulder, but stopped himself a half inch from her bare skin. She startled so easily that the touch of his tongue would probably evoke a shriek of alarm, and she might—accidentally—sock him in the nose. Or he might—intentionally—decide to quiet her with a kiss.

And that way lay madness. She wasn't the woman for him, wasn't even close. She was just the woman who happened to be with him; the woman who—without his permission or consent—had enmeshed him in her problems, gotten him kidnapped, stripped and robbed, nearly had seduced him in a damned haystack, then all but reduced him to a soprano with one random, knee-jerk reaction. And she'd done it all by accident.

He ought to be furious. He ought to be incensed at the demolition of his wedding plans. He ought to be enraged at being kidnapped, shot at and humiliated. He should not be sitting here, watching Eliza and wallowing in the mystifying attraction she aroused in him.

Mystifying?

Hell, there was no mystery about what he was feeling. She was as naked as he was. That accounted for the attraction. He might be a Cortland, but he was as susceptible to fantasy as the next man. Put him naked in a haystack with any woman and...

He straightened and dragged his gaze away from her. He had spent too much time looking at her already. It was time to... The temptation was too great, and his gaze slid slowly back to her satiny skin, while his thoughts skidded over the edge into the danger zone once again.

And once again, he jerked them back in line with reality. He should not still be here, looking at her, thinking about the taste of her lips, fantasizing, lusting....

He had to get out of this haystack before he forgot what happened when she was startled and kissed her, anyway. Maybe later he could make sense of his reluctance to leave her and this fusty, uncomfortable mound of straw. And maybe later he'd take time to think about why he wasn't angry about the chaos she'd created in his life. But for now, he was going to do what he should have done in the beginning—concentrate on getting some clothes and some assistance, hopefully in that order.

All he needed was a direction—north, south, east or west. Where was the most likely location for a farmhouse in relation to a haystack? He narrowed his gaze on the abandoned barn and caught sight of the yellow dog. Eliza's werewolf. He didn't know much about canines, but this one looked fat and friendly, familiar with his surroundings. He undoubtedly belonged to some nice family in the area. And if Mack could follow him home...

He slid across the slippery hay and pushed himself to his feet. With a last, tender look at Eliza, nestled in the hay like Little Boy Blue—only without the blue—he brushed the tendrils of straw from his skin and scratched a couple of persistent itches. He walked closer to the barn, then whistled softly and called to the dog. "Home, Wolfman. Go home, boy. Home. Food. You know, dinner. Or breakfast. A midnight snack. Something to eat. Are you hungry, old boy?"

With a doggy grin and a floppy wave of his tail, the dog trotted across the field, clearly understanding at least one word of the request and just as clearly inviting Mack to tag along.

"IF YOU THINK I'm going over another barbed-wire fence, you are stupider than you look." Mack scowled at the big, friendly dog he had followed across one flat field after another. He might as well have stayed in the haystack with Eliza for all the progress he'd made finding help. If he had stayed, he wouldn't be suffering from a hundred different aches and pains right now, either. As it was, he was scraped, scratched, bruised and dirty, and his feet couldn't hurt any worse if he'd walked four miles on a bed of nails. To add insult to injury, he hadn't seen so much as a tree stump to sit on in the whole time he'd followed the stupid dog.

"Some guide you are," he said to the lop-eared mutt. "After all this time, there's still not a farmhouse in sight. And I trusted you, too."

The dog barked a sharp encouragement, then trotted off again, his yellow tail waving like an ostrich feather above the stalks of half-grown wheat. Mack looked in every direction, wishing he had some idea of where he was in relation to the rest of the world. The barn, the haystack—every point of reference he'd had was lost in the seemingly endless fields of hay and wheat. For all he knew, he'd been circling the same territory over and over, going from the hay field to the wheat field and back again, following that sorry excuse of a farm dog. Well, he wasn't going to fight with another barbed-wire fence, that was for certain.

Determined, he set off along the fence line and at an angle to the dog's path through the wheat. When this was over, he was going to report that animal to the S.P.C.A. And the Lassie fan club, too.

ELIZA OPENED her eyes and bolted upright. Her heart pounding, her mind hovering between dreaming and wakefulness, she realized she was in unfamiliar surroundings. And she was alone. Outside. In the dark. And her dress was gone.

No, wait, that was the dream. She'd been wearing a wedding dress made of straw, but a tornado came and blew the dress away and left her sitting in a haystack. Her tension eased with her softly exhaled sigh. What a stupid dream. Why would she be dreaming about a haystack?

She yawned, stretched and froze as the rustle of hay accompanied her movements. Her fingers clenched and brought up a handful of straw. She *was* in a haystack. She raised her head and looked down at her nude body. Her dress *was* gone.

Million-dollar gown. Limousine. Mack. Chuck. Kidnapped. Barn. Jumper cables. Haystack. Kiss. The associative flashes of memory brought her fully awake and she turned around to locate Mack. It didn't take five seconds to conclude that he was long gone. He'd hardly even left an impression in the hay beside her. So where was he? And why had he let her go to sleep, anyway? He knew she didn't want to be left behind. He could have waited.

But men like MacKenzie Cortland didn't wait around for women like her. The minute she'd dozed off, he'd headed for civilization. She hoped he'd avoided the road, but that was probably exactly where he had gone. And he'd probably flagged down a car and gotten a ride, despite her warning about hitchhiking.

A flicker of anxiety slid down her spine at the thought. What if he had gotten picked up by some maniac? Why, at this very moment, he could be tied up in some secluded farmhouse while some maniac farmer sharpened his ax. Wait. She was being silly. Farmers were nice, helpful people. If Mack had hitched a ride with one of them, he was most likely sitting in a cozy farmhouse kitchen right now, eating fried chicken and drinking real milk drawn straight from a real cow.

Her stomach growled with envy. How could he be stuffing his face and clogging his arteries with butterfat while she was out here, waiting for him to remember where he'd left her? Maybe he didn't intend to come back for her. Maybe he was already on his way back to Kansas City. No, he wouldn't leave without her.

Her shoulders and her spirits drooped. Of course he would. Look what she'd done to him. He could have been—should have been—on his honeymoon at this very minute with the woman he loved. With Leanne. On a train.

Unwarranted jealousy attacked her and she scoffed at her silliness. She knew that if she were ever engaged to a man like Mack, she wouldn't consider spending even one night—and especially not the first night of her married life—on a train bound for Miami. The whole idea lacked flair, romance. In her opinion, it lacked everything except a sense of humor.

But this was no laughing matter. Her opinion didn't count, and she had absolutely no business thinking about Mack's honeymoon . . . even though it was her fault he'd missed it. She had no business thinking about him in any context, because he was practically married . . . although he had kissed her. And meant it.

And not just because he couldn't think of any other
way to shut her up.

Eliza sighed and lifted her chin. Well, Mack was
gone, and she wasn't going to sit around, waiting to be
rescued like some helpless damsel in distress. Tilting
her head to listen, she tried to distinguish just one
man-made sound in the night noises all around her.
But she couldn't hear so much as a distant rumble of
traffic, and the horizon wasn't outlined by the dull
haze of electric lights. She frowned, concluding that
civilization had to be a stiff walk in any direction.

Pursing her mouth in a contemplative pout, she
tried to imagine Mack striding barefoot and confi-
dent across the field in search of a farmhouse. But the
only image she could conjure in her mind's eye was of
his nice, tight end spotlighted by a moonbeam as he
walked down the dark, dirt road in search of a ride to
the nearest town. One thing was certain, at least. He'd
gone to get help, leaving her behind because he
thought it was the safest place for her to be. If she
waited, he'd be back. Or he'd send someone for her.

But she wasn't good at waiting. She wanted a drink
and something to eat. And a bath. She definitely
wanted a bath. And if Mack could find his way to
civilization in the dark, then, by golly, she ought to be
able to find a simple, little farmhouse.

THE HOUSE SAT like a snub nose on a flat face. It was
boxy and small, and if it had been painted black instead of white, Mack might have walked past and
never known it was there. His hand resting on a post
of the barbed-wire fence, he paused to study the angle of the roof, the darker shadows of the outbuildings and the silver T of a clothesline pole in the

backyard. He was going to have to cross the fence and a pasture to get to it, but the farmhouse was, at least, an affirmation that he was still in the good old U.S.A. and not the Twilight Zone.

At least, he hoped it was an affirmation. More than that, he hoped he'd be greeted with food, clothing and compassion, and not the subtle, deadly insanity of a Stephen King character.

He allowed himself a fleeting thought of Eliza, safe and sleeping in the haystack, and hoped that whatever nice, helpful farmer resided in this house would know by Mack's description exactly how to find her. Squaring his shoulders, he faced the fence, gingerly spread the top and middle wires and courageously put one leg through the opening.

With a friendly bark, the yellow dog dashed past on the other side, his tongue lolling from his mouth, his tail waving like a starter flag. Mack maintained his concentration and miraculously got through the fence and into the pasture without inflicting any further injury on his aching body. The dog barked again and raced ahead like Rin Tin Tin leading the soldiers to the enemy camp. "You don't fool me," Mack said, hobbling after him. "You were just as lost as I was."

The dog vanished around a shed in the middle of the pasture and started barking. A moment later, two distinctly bovine shadows trotted out from behind the building, herded by the yellow dog. Good thing Eliza wasn't with him, Mack thought. One good snuffle from either one of those cows and she'd be shrieking her head off.

He kept an eye on the cows as he drew even with the shed, but they were preoccupied with the yellow dog, which bounded around them, barking and nipping at their heels.

"Stop that, you idiot." Mack spoke sharply to the dog. "Not that you don't deserve to get kicked, but at least let me get out of this pasture before you get them really riled."

The dog continued to bark, and the cows gave a few aggravated snorts. The kind of low, threatening snorts Mack had heard at a rodeo once...just before a Brahma bull charged a clown in a barrel. But the dumb dog kept barking. The aggravated snorts became low, angry bellows, and Mack took off like a gimpy sprinter, racing for the safety zone outside the cow pasture.

There was a cattle gate in the barbed-wire fence, and he leapt onto it and climbed over, wincing as his hands and feet pressed down on the rough metal bars. The gate creaked under his weight, but he pushed himself up and over and landed with a bone-jarring thud on the other side. He bent over, grasping his knees for balance and gasping for breath.

Something wet smacked him on the back of the leg, and he wheeled around to see the yellow dog sitting there, a big, dumb grin on his doggy lips. Mack refused to smile back. "You are a nuisance. Go away. I can handle everything from here on in."

The dog's tail thumped the ground before he trotted off to investigate the two outbuildings behind the farmhouse.

Mack wiped the dog slobber off the back of his leg and, with an assessing glance at the farmyard, moved toward the nearest outbuilding. A few steps later he realized it was a chicken coop, enclosed in a wire mesh cage. A few more steps revealed, through sound and smell, that the other outbuilding was a pigpen.

He carefully negotiated the area between the two, trying not to breathe too deeply and inhale an overdose of the pungent odor. He stopped upwind of the livestock pens to study the back of the house, taking a moment to consider his approach.

If he walked right up to the door and knocked, he ran the risk of scaring the people inside and getting himself shot as an intruder. On the other hand, if he waited around until sunrise, Chuck would have several hours head start and Eliza would have even less chance of recovering the wedding gown. But a naked man at the back door in this part of the Bible Belt wasn't likely to be greeted with a grin and a "Howdy, stranger, come on in," regardless of what time of day or night he knocked.

Mack shifted from one throbbing foot to the other, debating the wisest course of action and wishing there was a pair of pants hanging on the clothesline. But even in the uncertain moonlight, he could see that not so much as a dishcloth had been left out overnight. He glanced over his shoulder at the chicken yard, wondering if he could collect enough stray feathers to construct a decent loincloth.

He glanced at the other building, thinking he could probably get enough mud from the sty to cover his body. But that wouldn't exactly conceal the fact that he had no clothes on, it would just make him smell like a pig.

Probably the best plan was to use his hands as a cloaking device and throw himself on the mercy of whoever opened the door. After all, it would be readily apparent that he wasn't concealing a weapon.

Squaring his shoulders, he headed for the farm-house.

VANGIE KEPT HER BIFOCALS, a romance novel, an alarm clock and an iron skillet on the bedside table. The glasses and the novel were there because she liked to read every night before going to sleep. The clock was there just in case she overslept...which hadn't happened in twenty-two years. The skillet was there as a handy weapon against intruders...although she had yet to need it, either.

Most warm nights she slept with the windows open, so Mr. Silk could come and go as he pleased. But lately that big yellow dog had been sniffin' round the hen-house, and she didn't want her Mr. Silk, her sweet lit-tle Yorkie, messin' with that filthy derelict. So she kept the windows cracked an inch or two, kept the electric fan running and got up as necessary during the night to let Mr. Silk outside to do his deed.

He never gave her no trouble, either. Just trotted outside to the far end of the clothesline, did his busi-ness, then trotted back. Mr. Silk was as good as gold and he never whined to go out unless he had a need to—like now. Squinting at the clock, which said 10:50 p.m., Vangie threw back the covers, thrust her feet into her bedroom slippers and grabbed the skillet out of habit.

Scuffing her way through the dark kitchen to the back door, she realized halfway there that she'd left her glasses on the bedside table. She couldn't see real good without them, but she'd lived in this house nigh on forty-eight years and reckoned she could make it to the back door all right without the bifocals.

When she opened the door and pushed open the screen, Mr. Silk growled deep in his throat, then rushed out in a frenzy of furious yapping. Wishing she hadn't forgotten to put on her spectacles, Vangie squinted in a vain attempt to see across the yard. She could just make out something light colored moving past the chicken house, and she knew in her heart that old yellah dog was after her layin' hens again. And her dear Mr. Silk was out there, doin' his eight-pound best to save 'em.

Setting the skillet on the countertop, she reached behind the door for the air rifle she always kept there. Then, without a second's hesitation, she used her foot to wedge open the screen door, raised the air rifle to her shoulder and aimed it in the direction of the henhouse.

Chapter Eight

One minute the farmyard was as peaceful as a Rockwell painting. The next minute it erupted in a torrent of noisy activity straight out of the Keystone Cops. Mack barely had time to realize the back door of the house was opening before he was under siege by a squeaking hair ball that flew around his ankles in a frenzied blur of nipping and yapping. Behind him, the chicken coop came alive, as chickens were startled out of their roost and into a crescendoing squawk by the yellow dog, which had found a way under the chicken wire and was now having a whopping good time in the henhouse. The porkers snuffed and snorted at being rudely awakened, and Mack let out a choked "Ow!" as the hair ball got a grip on his toe.

As he leaned down to rescue his extremity, he heard a *whisssssttt* and felt something streak through the air across his bent, bare back. A pinging sound came from the tin roof of the pigsty, and with the snarling wad of fur clamped in his hand, he straightened and spun around in alarm...as a second *whisssssttt* snapped past him at hip height.

"Hey!" he yelled, but his protest was no match for the barking yellow dog, the squawking chickens, the snorting pigs and the faint but fearful sound of a rifle being cocked.

"Get out of my henhouse, you yellow son of Satan!"

Whisssttt! Ping!

A BB gun, Mack thought as the pellet zinged past him and struck the tin roof of the chicken coop. Some damn fool was shooting at him with a BB gun. "Hey!" he yelled again, whirling to face the shooter.

Whisssttt! Ping! "I'm gonna teach you a lesson you ain't never gonna forget, you mangy chicken thief!"

Whisssttt! Ping!

"Stop! Don't shoot! I'm holding your dog!" He pitched his voice above the fray and self-protectively lowered the yapping Yorkie into service as a fig leaf and shield. "And I'm not a chicken thief."

There was a moment of reckoning, a cease-fire hardly recognizable amid the barnyard frenzy and then the cold, calculating click of the cocking lever.

"You put Mr. Silk down, stranger, or I swear I'll shoot your eye out."

Mack looked down and met a ferocious, beady-eyed glare. "Mr. Silk?" he said skeptically, and the tiny dog with a topknot bared his teeth, growling like a grizzly bear.

Whisssttt! This time the pellet zipped past Mack's ear, but missed hitting either of the outbuildings.

"I ain't whistling Dixie, stranger," the woman called in a voice that meant business. "Now, put my dog down."

"I will," he said quickly. "I'll do it, but first I need to tell you—"

"You ain't in no position to bargain, Mister. Put him down!"

Mack debated for maybe half a second, while Mr. Silk's growl grew into an ominous rattle. Then, holding the dog a careful distance from his all-too-vulnerable body, he bent to set down the Yorkie. But the closer they got to the ground, the fiercer the growl became.

"I'm not going to hurt you, fuzz ball." He stopped in midbend and tried to soothe the dog, but knew immediately he was wasting his breath on the ill-tempered Mr. Silk. He raised his voice and aimed it at the house. "He doesn't seem to *want* down, ma'am."

Whisssttt! A sharp sting on his thigh followed the whine of the BB. "Yeowwww!" Mack's muscles clenched and he lost his balance and toppled backward onto the ground, striking his tailbone. He rubbed his smarting thigh with one hand as he held the snarling Yorkie at arm's length with the other. "Are you crazy, lady?"

"That's for me to know and you to find out, now, ain't it?"

He didn't need to find out. He needed to get out of firing range. To that end, he released his hold on the cantankerous Mr. Silk and rolled over, scrambling onto his hands and knees and crawling as fast as he could toward the pigsty and shelter. The little Yorkie came after him, yapping incessantly and darting in and out, nipping at his ankle.

With a playful bark, the yellow dog deserted the henhouse to take part in this new and intriguing game. He crawled under the chicken wire, bounded across the yard like a puppy chasing a stick and skidded to a halt directly in Mack's path.

"Get out of the way, you idiot!" Mack waved, and the yellow dog jumped from side to side, barking continuously, clearly delighted that Mack wanted to play.

Mr. Silk, on the other hand—or rather, on the other ankle—was clearly frustrated that his quarry would not roll over and die. Apparently he was none too happy with the appearance of the yellow dog, either, for he emitted a series of warning yaps and stiff-legged jumps before renewing his attack on Mack's foot. Mack reached back and grabbed the Yorkie by the scruff of the neck, transforming the little fur ball into a frenzy of gnashing teeth and vicious barking.

The yellow dog came closer, sticking out his nose and getting it nipped for his trouble. He drew back, startled, then growled menacingly. Mr. Silk returned the threat threefold.

"Well, hell!" Much as he wanted to, Mack couldn't just drop the little spitfire. The Yorkie didn't deserve to end up as an after-chicken-dinner mint for the stupid yellow dog. Mack assessed the urgency of his situation, glancing over his shoulder at the shadowed farmhouse, then ahead at the proximity of the pigpen, then at one snarling dog and then the other.

Old Yeller moved a threatening inch closer, and Mack scuttled to the side to keep the two dogs from making contact. The growling intensified, both behind him and at the end of his arm, and suddenly he wondered what he thought he was doing, standing—crouching, actually—between the bite of reality and the tough-guy illusions of Mr. Silk.

"I *told* you to put down my dog." The woman's voice whipped into the backyard arena like a blast from a referee's whistle. "If I hav'ta call the sheriff, you're gonna be real sorry."

"Please!" he yelled back as he wrestled to keep the Yorkie's teeth from sinking into his hand. "Call the damned sheriff!"

Whisssssttt!

He jumped as the pellet zipped past his ear.

"You watch your language, Mister!"

That did it. He was going to stand up and walk out of this nightmare. And if she shot him again, he would damn well sue her. "Lady, if you don't put that blasted BB gun away, *I'm* going to call the sheriff! Do you understand?"

Apparently she did, because he heard the now-familiar click of the cocking lever. Like a rat running for an alley, Mack scurried toward the pigpen, deciding he'd continue negotiations from behind a building. Any building.

Whisssttt! Ping!

"Yap—yap—yap—yap—yap!" Mr. Silk yipped in staccato accompaniment to Mack's jogging steps.

Whisssttt! Ping!

At the side of the pigpen, Mack slipped on a muddy patch, but caught the wall with one hand and kept going until he rounded the corner. Behind the pigsty, he sank to the ground, held up a startled and suddenly silent Mr. Silk by the scruff of the neck and stared him down. "You're free to go, Champ, but if you make one move toward my ankle, you're history. Got it?"

Tough guy to the end, the Yorkie growled back, spoiling for a fight. When the yellow dog trotted around the corner of the building, Mr. Silk's threat became a challenging yip, yip, yip, and he squirmed, ready to brawl. Deciding it wasn't his night to protect hair balls from extinction, Mack let him go. In seconds, the two dogs were circling each other like boxers in a ring, waiting to see which one would throw the first punch.

Mack rubbed his forehead, realizing too late that he had smeared the stinky mud from his hand onto his face. He wiped it off as best he could with the back of his hand and then ran his palm down the side of the pigsty to get rid of the worst of the dirt . . . and winced as a nail head gouged his thumb. "Damn." He stuck his thumb in his mouth, tasted a nasty mixture of mud and blood, and then tried to scrape the taste from his tongue and spit it out. Was there anything else that could possibly go wrong in one night?

"Yoo-hoo!" The call came from the direction of the pasture, and his heart leapt with sudden, glad recognition . . . just before it sank with dread at the recollection that every time Eliza was near something painful happened to him. And he was in enough pain already.

"Yoo-hoo! Anybody home?"

He strained to see her in the darkness, but she was on the other side of the fence and . . . The pasture. She was in the pasture with the snuffling cows. "Eliza," he called. "Go back! Get out of the pasture!"

"Mack?" She sounded pleased, even at a distance. "Is that you, Mack?"

"Eliza, get out of there!"

"What?" she yelled back. "What did you say?"

"Go back! There's a crazy woman with a BB gun over here and there are cows in the—"

"I knew you was up to no good," the sharpshooter's voice interrupted.

Mack turned his head and blinked in the sudden, blinding beam of a flashlight. "I beg your pardon?"

Dropping his hands to the ground, he started to push himself to his feet.

"*Don't* make a move, Mister, unlessen' I tell you to."

The woman's command stopped him an inch off the ground and he hesitated, bracing his weight on his hands and feet as he squinted in the glare of the flashlight. At this range, she probably could shoot his eye out, and he wasn't taking any chances. "Please," he began. "Let me explain."

"Mack?" Eliza called, sounding concerned and cautious, even across a half acre of cow pasture. "What's going on down there? Did you get in the house?"

"Run, Eliza!" he yelled back. "Get out of—"

"Aha!" the woman said. "Just like I thought. You and your partner was plannin' to break into my house, weren't ya? I read the newspapers. I know the sick things goin' on in the world. I'll bet the two of you make Bonnie and Clyde look like the Lennon Sisters."

He stared at the blinding light in stunned protest. "You're got this all—"

And then one of the cows bellowed a long, agitated, "*Moooo.*"

"*Aaaaah!*" Eliza screamed. "*Aaaaah! Aaaaah!*"

Barking like a maniac, the yellow dog raced around the corner of the pigpen and jumped Mack in his wild dash toward the pasture. Like a pint-size sidekick, Mr. Silk skimmed under Mack's upraised knees and sprinted after the other dog.

"Mr. Silk!" the woman shouted, following the Yorkie with the flashlight beam. "Come back, Mr. Silk!"

As the flashlight beam did a double-take and moved back across the ground toward him, Mack stayed where he was, caught between the urge to laugh hysterically and the profound desire to vanish off the face of the earth. He stared up at the tiny, but fierce-looking gray-haired woman who stood over him.

Her myopic eyes followed the beam as it traveled past his toes and up his legs to fasten on his prominently displayed masculinity. She leaned over closer to him and he quickly sat, drawing his knees to his chest and trying his best to look casual.

The woman gasped. "Gawd Amighty," she whispered. "You must be some kind of pervert."

He barely had time to think that this had been one hell of a night before he saw the shine on a Teflon-coated frying pan as it caught a glimmer of moonlight above his head.

And then everything went black.

"MACK? Mack? Please, wake up, Mack." Eliza's voice floated through the drumbeat inside his head and he struggled toward it.

"He's coming around," someone said, and in Mack's foggy brain, a stream of unrelated words spun around and around and around.

"She'll be comin' round the mountain when she comes," he said in a strange, singsongy voice that trailed off to a feeble, "Toot, toot."

"Mack, wake up." It was Eliza again.

"He's hallucinatin'," the other voice said.

"You'd hallucinate, too, if you'd gotten hit over the head with a frying pan." Eliza sounded upset, and Mack fought to open his eyelids.

"Well, little lady, you can just count your lucky stars Miz Vangie didn't hit him any harder or he might have somethin' worse than a possible concussion."

Mack felt Eliza's hand on his forehead and heard her ask, "How much longer before the doctor gets here?"

"Oh, maybe five, ten minutes. What time did you call the doc, Tim?"

"Me? I thought you called him."

"Doggone it, Tim, I told you to call the doc."

"Well, Jim, you're the sheriff. You're 'sposed to make the calls."

"And you're the deputy. You're 'sposed to do what I tell ya. Now, go on and call the doc."

"I don't see why I have to be the one to do it. If I was the sheriff, you'd say I was the one supposed to make the calls."

"Yeah, well, it's not your turn to be sheriff, and I get to say who does what, so go on and call the doc."

"It's nearly midnight, and you know how Doc hates gettin' called out after eleven. That's why you want me to do it."

"Is not."

"Oh, for heaven's sake." Eliza's hand stopped stroking Mack's forehead, and he missed her soothing touch. "*I'll* call. Where's the phone?"

"In the kitchen. Miz Vangie'll tell you the number."

"All right." Eliza moved away. "If anything happens to him while I'm in the other room, I'm holding you both responsible. Understand?"

"Oh, he'll be fine, ma'am. Don't you worry. Me and Jim'll watch him like hawks."

Mack opened one eye and saw two—three—four faces swimming through the space over his head. Two pairs of frowns and two unfamiliar sets of eyes blurred together and apart, together and apart, in a dizzy spin of distorted, but identical images. He closed his eye and gathered the fortitude to take a second look.

"Maybe we should pour some water on him. See if that'll wake him up."

Mack tried again, forcing up one eyelid and then the other, slowly bringing into focus the faces that hovered over his head like reflections in a fun-house mirror. After skewing his eyes into varying degrees of a squint, he still couldn't clear up his double vision.

"Hello." One of the faces suddenly loomed closer. "See, Jim, I told ya he was comin' around."

Mack's vision blurred again, then came into focus on two identical faces. "Twins?" he muttered. "Is there... two of you?"

"You're as sharp as a steak knife, stranger," one of the men said. "I'm Sheriff Jim Cooper and this here's my twin brother, Deputy Tim Cooper."

"But at twelve a.m., I'll be Sheriff Cooper," Deputy Tim said importantly. "Me and Jim alternate between bein' the sheriff and the deputy like that 'cause the vote was evenly divided, and so we just split the job right down the middle. Twenty-four hours as sheriff, twenty-four hours as deputy. You must be feelin' better."

Mack ran his tongue over his dry lips. "Better than what?"

A gruff smile showed up on one face and was quickly echoed on the other. "You look like you've had a mighty rough night, doesn't he, Jim?"

"He does for sure, Tim. Course, I wouldn't want to be on the wrong end of Miz Vangie's air rifle when she commenced to firin', would you?"

"Nope, not me, Jim. She could shoot a man's eye out with that gun of hers. You know, you're real lucky, Mr.—?"

Mack didn't think he ought to supply his full name to anyone just yet, least of all to two county officials who were so doggone proud of Miz Vangie's rifle skills. His vision was getting better, and he focused on the hint of sparkle in the ceiling plaster overhead. "Where am I?" he asked. "And where did Eliza go?"

"She went to call the doc. And you're on Miz Vangie's sofa in Miz Vangie's livin' room. She caught you trying to break into her house, and she hit you with a fryin' pan. Then she called the law."

"The law. That's me and Jim."

"I wasn't trying to break in," Mack said.

"Yeah, that's what Eliza told us," Deputy Jim—or Tim—said. "She explained everything."

Mack's headache took on a whole new level of discomfort. "She . . . explained?"

"Yeah. Hell of a way to spend your weddin' night."

"Yeah. Bummer of a honeymoon." The twin sheriffs chuckled. "It's a good thing Eliza was able to talk Miz Vangie out of pressin' charges, though. She was pretty durn upset when we got here."

"Eliza?"

"Miz Vangie. You dang near scared her to death."

"I scared *her?*" Mack was as incredulous as his pounding headache would allow. "She *shot* me! Did she tell you that? Here, I can show you the bruise." He pushed at the light blanket covering his body, but it just tangled around his thighs. Exasperated, he lifted his head, looked down and realized with a sinking heart that there was no blanket covering him. He was wearing a lady's nightgown. A bibbed-and-tucked, rosebud-print, lace-trimmed, flannel lady's nightgown.

He lifted his hand to rub his forehead and had to bat the ruffled sleeve away from his nose and mouth. With a low groan, he swung his feet to the floor and fought off a sudden wave of dizziness. "What is this?" He plucked at a flannel rosebud. "And how did it get on me?"

"Miz Vangie is a maiden lady, you know, and you gave her quite a shock. So yer wife took care of coverin' you up before me and Tim arrived." The twins chuckled again, a kind of guffaw in stereo. "She said she'd already seen you naked so it was all right."

"My wife?" he repeated through a haze of aches and pains. "Did I get married?"

"Don't you remember?"

He shook his head and massaged his temples. "I thought I was kidnapped."

"Marriage can feel like that, but it usually takes more than a few hours."

"I need a drink."

"Miz Vangie's cookin' up some cocoa now."

Cocoa. Oh, terrific. "Would you ask her to add about half a bottle of Scotch?"

Tim—and Jim—looked properly aghast at the idea. "We can't drink on duty."

Mack rested his head in his hands. "Don't worry. I'll drink yours."

One of the men leaned down and patted Mack on the back. "Alcohol won't solve nothin'. You got to face your problems and sock 'em in the nose."

Mack eyed the burly sheriff and his equally burly deputy, noting that the only obvious difference between them was the size of their badges. "Easy for you guys to say. You're not wearing a nightgown."

The deputy grinned. "Well, now, it looks right pretty on you. And it fits you a sight better than one of those gowns you'll be gettin' when you check into the county hospital."

"Hospital?" That was a scary thought. "I am not going to the hospital."

"Well, now," Deputy Tim said. "We'll just have to wait an' see what Doc says, won't we?"

"Is there some *reason* you don't want to go to the hospital?" the sheriff asked.

He could think of several reasons to stay out of this county's hospital, but he didn't think stating them would win him any brownie points with "the law." "I just want to go back and start this day over."

"There you go, wishin' your life away." Deputy Tim smiled and scratched behind his ear. "And your weddin' day at that."

The sheriff frowned as he propped one shiny black boot on the edge of Miz Vangie's sofa and leaned closer to Mack. "What I want to know is, if you could go back, what would you do that'd be different?"

"What I want to know, Jim Cooper, is what your nasty old boot is doing on my good furniture."

Sheriff Jim got his boot on the floor in a flash and looked as guilty as a kid with a slingshot. "Sorry, Miz Vangie. I was questionin' our boy here and forgot where I was for a minute."

The little gray-haired woman in the doorway nodded a stern acquittal before she entered the room and set the tray she carried on the coffee table in front of Mack. "So," she said. "You're awake."

"No thanks to you. You tried your best to kill me."

"I was protectin' my property as the United States Constitution says I have a right to." Miz Vangie gave him a dour look as she chose a coffee mug off the tray and held it out to him. "Drink this. I put somethin' in it for your headache."

He took the mug and eyed it suspiciously. The steam curled off the cocoa like a crooked finger, beckoning him to take a sip... just a sip. He wondered if arsenic had an aroma. "Where's Eliza?"

"I left her in the kitchen."

"What's she doing in there?"

"Huntin' for somethin' to eat." Miz Vangie settled on the edge of a rocking chair, looking remarkably like a parakeet about to fall off its perch. "She asked me if I minded and I told her she should just make herself at home, so I reckon that's what she's doin'."

It figured. He got shot, knocked unconscious and possibly poisoned, while Eliza got to "make herself at home." "Look," he said. "If I can just borrow a car, I'll get out of here and—"

"You had just as well forget that idea." Deputy Tim edged closer to the coffee table as the aroma of hot chocolate wafted up. "You're not goin' anywhere until the doc says you're able. Boy, this sure smells good." He picked a mug off the tray. "Don't you want a cup of Miz Vangie's cocoa, Sheriff Jim?"

"Don't mind if I do." The sheriff picked up the last mug with a nod of appreciation to Miz Vangie, who made room in her lap for a surly looking Mr. Silk. "Tim's right, Mack, and even if Doc says you're able, you couldn't drive anyway 'cause you don't have a driver's license. Me and Tim—bein' the law and all—we're honor bound not to let you get behind the wheel of a car unless you have a valid license."

Mack's head continued to pound and he decided it really didn't make much difference what Miz Vangie had put in his cocoa. "I'm a licensed driver," he said after the first sip. "Can't you call up my DMV record or something?"

Deputy Tim licked a cocoa mustache off his upper lip. "Could, but wouldn't do you any good."

"Why not?"

"Well, for one thing, you don't have a speck of identification. For all me and Jim know, you could be a notorious criminal usin' a fictitious name."

"Eliza will vouch for me."

Sheriff Jim shook his head. "For all we know, she could be a notorious criminal, too." The twins traded grins. "She wasn't exactly carrying much in the way of identification, either."

Mack didn't like the way they were grinning, and he certainly didn't like the hint of lechery in their expressions. "Our clothes were stolen," he said pointedly.

"Yeah."

"We heard."

The men chuckled and raised their mugs as if they had choreographed and timed their response.

"Look, I'm sure Eliza told you about the dress and being kidnapped and—"

"*Kidnapped?*" Miz Vangie tilted forward in the rocker, forcing Mr. Silk to poke out his head like a joey in a kangaroo's pocket. "She didn't tell me you *kidnapped* her!"

"Kidnapped?" Sheriff Jim frowned.

"That would be a serious offense." Deputy Tim set his mug on the table. "We'd have to put you in jail for that."

"Deputy Cooper..." Mack set his mug beside Deputy Tim's "...*I* was the victim."

"She kidnapped *you?*" Miz Vangie whisked the rocker into motion and the Yorkie slid off her lap. He shook himself and jumped onto the sofa next to Mack. "That is not what she told us," Miz Vangie continued. "She said today was your weddin' day."

Sheriff Jim's frown tightened with suspicion. "He said he doesn't remember gettin' married."

"Well, that's an odd thing not to remember."

The three of them looked at one another, then turned to eye Mack, clearly suspicious.

"I'm telling you the truth," he said. "Today was my wedding day, but I was kidnapped."

Miz Vangie pursed her lips. "This is beginnin' to sound mighty peculiar to me."

"Me, too." The sheriff hooked his thumbs over his belt. "It sounds to me like *someone* is lyin'."

Mack frowned. "Why would I lie to you?"

"To get out of going to jail, maybe?"

"Mack! Darling!" Eliza rushed into the room, a blue flannel nightgown plumped with air from her movements, her arms outstretched as if she'd been searching for him half of her life. "You're all right!" She flung herself onto the sofa and into his arms, accidentally trapping Mr. Silk in the folds of Mack's nightgown. The dog nipped him on the thigh.

"Ow," he said...except Eliza was kissing him, and his discomfort got swept away under the warm, sweet pressure of her mouth. He wrapped an arm around her shoulders and used his other hand to push the Yorkie off the couch. Then he concentrated on Eliza's kiss, deciding he should savor whatever moments of pleasure dropped into his lap.

She stroked his hair, his face, and kissed her way to his earlobe. "Let me do the talking," she whispered before her voice rose to a normal speaking tone. "Oh, my precious darling. I was so worried. Are you sure you don't want to lie down? You look so pale. Do you feel all right? Did you drink your cocoa?"

He stared at her, unable to fathom what she was up to.

"Eliza?" Miz Vangie said sternly as she picked up Mr. Silk and dropped him in her lap. "You told us you and Mack eloped."

"We did." Eliza kept her arms looped about his neck and looked over her shoulder at Miz Vangie and the twins. "We eloped this afternoon. Didn't Mack tell you?"

Sheriff Jim crossed his arms over his badge. "He says he was kidnapped."

Eliza was silent for a moment, and when she turned to look at Mack again, he could see her eyes and mouth were rounded with false alarm. "Oh, my darling," she said. "You can't have forgotten our wedding... unless—unless that blow on the head gave you..." she paused for effect "...amnesia!"

He raised his eyebrows. "I remember you," he said distinctly.

Her shoulders sagged. "But not the ceremony at that little chapel outside of Lawrence? Oh, Mack, it was so beautiful. I can't believe you've forgotten."

"Are you sure I was there?"

She gave him a quick frown before she sighed— deeply and very audibly. "Oh, Mack, Mack, Mack,

Mack.'' Then she laid her head on his shoulder and whispered fiercely, ''Back me up. I'll explain later.'' Her head came up, almost clipping him on the chin, but he was too quick for her. ''Oh, Sheriff Jim and Deputy Tim,'' she said. ''What am I going to do? I'm afraid my husband has lost his mind.''

''Memory,'' Mack corrected, but no one paid any attention to him.

''Amnesia, huh?'' Deputy Tim stroked his chin. ''Did you hit him that hard, Miz Vangie?''

''I don't think so. I'm not near as strong as I used to be. And I wasn't tryin' to really hurt him, you know.''

In a glance, Mack assessed Miz Vangie's fragile appearance and felt grateful he hadn't met her in her prime.

''Well, now, me and Tim know that for sure, Miz Vangie.'' The sheriff stroked his chin in exact and unconscious imitation of his twin. ''But you musta packed more of a wallop than you meant to, 'cause he was still unconscious when we got here.''

''But that wasn't from me hittin' him with the skillet,'' Miz Vangie said. ''That was from Eliza bangin' his head on the door facin' when we carried him inside.''

Mack looked at Eliza.

''It was an accident,'' she said.

''I'm not surprised,'' he replied.

''Well, as the sheriff, I am just gonna have to get to the bottom of this.'' Jim hitched up his trousers. ''Now, were you kidnapped or weren't ya?''

''Yes,'' Mack stated firmly.

At the same moment, Eliza said a clear and definite, ''No.''

He looked at her with growing irritation. "Tell these people the truth, Eliza."

"I already tried that, Mack."

"Then tell them again."

She shrugged. "You really should have let me do the talking."

"Uh-oh." Tim rubbed the back of his neck. "I think we got ourselves a little problem."

"Someone sure does." Sheriff Jim looked from Mack to Eliza and back again. "Because if one of you was kidnapped and one of you is lyin' about it, then somewhere there's been a crime committed, and I got no choice but to lock one of you up until I can figure out what really happened."

"I just told you what happened," Mack said, ignoring Eliza's warning frown. "Eliza, please, just tell the truth. That's always the best policy, trust me."

She sighed and scooted off his lap. "We aren't married," she said. "There wasn't a wedding. He doesn't have amnesia. His shirt cuff got tangled in my sleeve and he left the woman he was supposed to marry on the church steps because Chuck kidnapped the million-dollar dress."

Miz Vangie stopped rocking and turned her myopic, but commanding gaze on the sheriff. "Jim, I think it's pretty clear what's going on here."

"Yes, Miz Vangie. You're right." Sheriff Jim's barrel chest expanded as he made another adjustment of his khaki pants. "And I'm gonna put a stop to it right now. Tim, get ahold of Doc and tell him to meet us at the jail." He reached down and grasped Mack's arm. "Come on, Mack, I'm placin' you under arrest."

Chapter Nine

"Now, you just get on in there and keep him company for a while. I'll be back to get you when everything's ready." Sheriff Cooper gave Eliza a wink as he closed the door, shutting her into the walkway between a double row of jail cells. She wrinkled her nose at the unsavory smell and blinked in the dingy light, but with a show of confidence, she straightened her shoulders and approached the first enclosure. Pressing her palms against the cool iron bars, she looked in at Mack, who was stretched out on a too-small cot in the six-by-nine-foot cell.

He had his arm draped over his eyes and was so still he might have been asleep. Except he wasn't. She knew no one could sleep through all the sheriff's bolt clanking, key jangling and very vocal instructions—even if Mack hadn't given any sign as yet that he was awake and aware of her presence. He just lay there, probably too angry with her to speak.

She sighed. Auntie Gem had always told her that one day she'd learn the value of staying out of trouble in the first place instead of trying to explain her way out of it afterward. She tucked a wayward strand of hair behind her ear and bravely lifted her chin. "One day" had arrived.

"Let me guess. You baked me a cake, but forgot to put the file inside."

She jumped a little at the hollow echo of his voice against the concrete-block walls. "I'm glad your funny bone is still in working order," she said with forced cheerfulness. She wished he'd get up off the cot or at least sit up and look at her. "Sheriff Cooper said the doc gave you a clean bill of health. No concussion or broken bones or anything major like that. How do you feel?"

"Like I was whacked off at the root and shoved headfirst through a hay baler."

His arm remained across his face...and she figured it was because he wasn't any too eager to set eyes on her again. "I see you got rid of the nightgown. You must be more comfortable in that."

"Oh, yes," he said dryly. "It's hard to understand why these state-issued jumpsuits aren't more popular with the general public. Do you think it could be the color?"

She pressed her lips together, reminding herself that he had not had a good day and was understandably not in the best of moods. "I find it hard to imagine that you look better in orange than you did in rosebud flannel, but if you'll get up and sashay around the cell a couple of times, I might change my mind."

"Flattery will get you nowhere, Eliza. It's going to take genuine groveling."

"How about a pardon?"

"As in you beg my pardon?"

"As in I think you're about to be reprieved."

His arm came away from his eyes, and she felt the impact of his questioning frown. "The charges have been dropped?"

"Mmm... that's what I understand, yes."

He stood up slowly, first swinging his legs off the cot and putting his feet on the floor, then bracing his hands on the thin edge of the mattress and pushing himself up. The jail-issue jumpsuit fit him better than Miz Vangie's nightgown had, but orange wasn't really his color. Or maybe it was the wary expression in his dark eyes that clashed with the clothes. Not that it made any difference. He was easily the most attractive man she'd ever seen... in jail-house orange or rosebud flannel.

Holding her gaze by sheer force of will, he took one solid step away from the cot and stopped a bare two inches from the cell bars she was standing in front of. "Okay, what's the catch?"

"Catch?" she asked, as if she couldn't imagine why he thought there might be a loophole.

"Come on, Eliza, give me the bottom line."

"I don't know, Mack. Really. Miz Vangie and the sheriff are being kind of secretive, whispering to each other and scurrying in and out. I can't say for sure what they're doing."

"Then how do you know they're going to release me?"

"I'm not sure they're going to release you...exactly. I think it's gonna be more along the lines of a, uh, custody transfer."

He placed his hands over hers on the bars, sending a quicksilver awareness flashing through her. "But Miz Vangie is dropping the indecent-exposure charge, right?"

"She feels just awful about what happened, Mack. Really. She wants to make it up to you."

"I'll just bet she does."

Eliza wished she could touch the corner of his mouth, ease the lines of tension there, explain to him that she hadn't meant to cause so much trouble. Or maybe she only wanted to distract him for a moment or two. "She let me borrow this outfit."

His gaze slid over her, taking in the ill-fitting pink shirtwaist, the lace-cuffed white anklets, the no-nonsense, laced-up shoes and the modest tint of pink on her lips. "Beautiful."

"Don't be patronizing. I know I look like I belong on the set of 'The Beverly Hillbillies.'"

"But you combed the hay out of your hair."

She shrugged. "Miz Vangie insisted."

"She's crazy. I thought the hay was a nice touch."

Eliza met his gaze for an instant, feeling a sweet, wistful warmth at the memory of being with him in the haystack. She thought she could see a hint of intimacy in his eyes, as if he remembered, too. But if it was there, it would vanish the moment she told him...

"I think she is, actually. Crazy, I mean. Truly, Mack, I tried to talk her out of this ridiculous idea, but I think she's going ahead with it, anyway."

His wary expression took a turn for the worse. "All right, what do I have to do to get out of here? Make a contribution to the twins' reelection campaign? Recommend Miz Vangie for a job with the CIA? What?"

"Nothing like that." Eliza gathered her courage and lost it again at the fateful moment of truth. "Miz Vangie's, uh, planning a little...surprise for you. For us."

"Surprise?"

"Oh, sort of a...party kind of surprise, I guess you could say."

He pursed his lips. "Are the Marx Brothers in on this little party surprise?"

"Well, one of them is. It's Tim's shift as sheriff. But he's on our side, at least more so than Jim...who's now the deputy and who still isn't convinced I'm telling the truth."

"Oh, no, don't tell me the truth has once again reared its ugly head."

"This is no laughing matter, Mack."

"Eliza, look at me. I'm behind bars. In jail. Me. Cortland and conservative to the bone. A man who doesn't even jaywalk. I am under arrest for being a pervert or a kidnapper or something equally heinous. Believe me, I am not laughing."

She twisted her hand around the bar until he stopped her with persuasive pressure. "Oh, Mack, if you'd just gone along with me on the elopement story, you wouldn't be in jail now and we wouldn't be in this mess. Or at least, it wouldn't have gotten any more complicated." She swallowed hard. "Maybe I'm wrong. Maybe they're really not out there planning what I think they're planning. And even if they are and worse comes to worst, I'm sure it can all be undone later. It would be easy to get a divorce when you didn't mean to get married, anyway, wouldn't it? And I did try to tell the truth in the very beginning. Really, I did. But you were unconscious and I was scared and—"

"Whoa." His grip on her hands tightened, pressing her palms against the iron bars and sending a wave of totally irrelevant, but very real, sensual response through her. "Who's getting married?" he asked slowly. "And who's getting divorced?"

She bit her lip. "Well, technically, I suppose, it would be an annulment."

"An annulment of what?"

"Marriage," she said bravely.

"Whose marriage?"

She wished he wasn't touching her, holding her palms against the cool metal, covering her with warmth. "Ours."

"Our marriage," he repeated, as if he had to hear the words aloud to clarify their meaning. "Ours? Yours and mine?"

"Yes."

He leaned closer to the bars and lowered his voice to a whisper. "Are we going to have to pretend to get an annulment of the marriage I'm supposed to have forgotten because of the amnesia?"

"We can't annul that marriage, Mack, because you convinced them that that wedding never happened."

"*I* convinced them? That's pretty amazing considering that these people haven't believed a single thing I've said."

"Exactly, which is why you should have let me do the talking instead of jumping in with the truth and confusing things."

"Well, excuse me. This has been a confusing day."

"Yes, and it isn't over yet."

"What does that mean?" He paused to consider. "The party? Is that it? Something's going to happen at the surprise party?" Comprehension and disbelief vied for jurisdiction over his expression. "No," he said. "Tell me they're not out there planning a wedding for us."

She bit her lip again. "I tried to explain it to them, Mack. Really I did. But since you blew my elopement story to smithereens, I had to come up with a whole different explanation to convince them you weren't lying and that you didn't belong in jail. Miz Vangie pounced on a few minor details and drew her own conclusions, and, well, to make a long story short, I just saw them sneaking a man with a clerical collar into the office."

His brow furrowed in a thunderous line and he released his hold on her hands. "What were those *few minor details*, Eliza?"

"There's no need to raise your voice." Her tone stayed level and low, even though she did step back from the bars. "I simply mentioned that you were late for your own wedding, and Miz Vangie sort of took over from there and came up with the idea that your family was forcing you to marry Leanne, but that you were really in love with me. But I wouldn't agree to elope with you because then you'd lose your family inheritance—which I inadvertently led her to believe is quite substantial—and I couldn't stand in the way of your future. And besides, Leanne is the perfect wife for you, while I, obviously, am not at all the kind of woman you need. But you couldn't bear the thought of living without me, so you kidnapped me. And...I really don't know where she got this part, Mack, because I certainly never said I was going to marry a man I didn't love just so you'd be forced to go ahead with your wedding to Leanne...but Miz Vangie thinks you kidnapped me only moments before I said 'I do' to this other guy and that you've been trying to persuade me to marry you ever since we drove away from the church."

Mack stared at her in awed silence.

Her palms began to sweat and she wiped them on the polished-cotton skirt. "Say something, Mack. Yell if you have to, but say something."

He opened his mouth, closed it, then shook his head in wonder. "*All that* came out of a statement about my being late for the wedding?"

"Well, most of it. I really am sorry. I was just trying to convince Miz Vangie and Tim and Jim that you're not a pervert and you don't belong in jail, and that it was totally my fault that you weren't wearing any clothes. The next thing I knew they stopped listening to me and started talking about how two people who were so eager to be together that they forgot where they lost their clothes and wound up rolling around in a haystack shouldn't be let loose without a marriage license."

"You told them we rolled in the haystack?"

She tossed him a rueful frown. "They added the hay in my hair to the hay in your hair and figured that one out for themselves."

He ran his fingers across his jaw. "So how are we going to get out of this?"

"I don't know. Maybe I could convince them we're part of an undercover sting operation and that we were trying to infiltrate a gang of nudist burglars."

"What?"

"It was a joke, Mack," she said, sighing. "A meager attempt to wipe the worry lines off your face. It won't happen again."

"I am not worried."

"Yes, you are, and I don't blame you a bit. I mean, how are you going to explain to Leanne that you accidentally had to marry me?"

"I'm not."

"Well, I don't think I can explain it to her."

He paced to the sink and back—four steps round-trip. "Do me a favor, Eliza. Don't explain anything else on my behalf. Please."

"You're right. Auntie Gem tried to warn me about this kind of misunderstanding."

"Misunderstanding?" he repeated in disbelief, shaking his head. "I think this *misunderstanding* belongs in the *Guinness Book of Records.* How could you have gotten things in such a sorry state?"

"It wouldn't be if you'd just trusted me a little."

He stared at her in amazement. "Did you expect me to sit there and nod my head while you persuaded these people I'd lost my mind? They'd have locked me up in a padded cell so fast it would have made even you dizzy."

"Memory," she corrected. "I never said you'd lost your mind."

"Yes, you did."

"No, I didn't."

He scowled at her.

She scowled back. "Frankly, under the circumstances, I don't think you could have come up with an explanation any better than my elopement story."

"I could have thought of some version of the truth that at least resembled what actually happened, something that would have sent the Cooper boys looking for Chuck and the dress instead of landing me in jail."

"The dress is the problem, Mack. I could have told Miz Vangie and the sheriff to call Mrs. Pageatt and verify that the gown was worth a lot of money, but then she'd have told them I stole the dress, and I wasn't sure I could convince them I hadn't. And if I was in jail, too, how would either of us get out? So that's why I didn't tell them. Besides, no one wants to believe the dress is worth a million dollars.''

"Chuck believed you right away."

Her chin came up. "Well, then, maybe you should just call him up and let *him* explain it."

"Can't. I've already used my one allotted phone call."

"You talked with an attorney?"

"No, I called Leanne, thinking she could call an attorney for me."

Eliza heard the fatigue in his voice and sensed that his anger with her was fading. "I guess help is on the way, then?"

He shrugged. "Leanne didn't stay on the line long enough for me to ask for help. Somewhere between my 'hello' and 'I can explain,' she hung up."

Her heart went out to him of its own accord and without restraint. "I'm sorry, Mack. You have been patient and kind and a complete gentleman since the first moment I met you, and I'm terribly sorry that your fiancée has such poor regard for your character."

The outer door opened before he could answer, but Eliza saw the surprise and appreciation in his eyes, and she smiled.

"We're ready," Miz Vangie said in a voice that wavered with excitement. "You are not going to believe this. You're really not going to believe this."

It *was* difficult to believe, Mack thought, as he stepped into the sheriff's office a few minutes later. A canopy of yellow crime-scene tape was draped from the center light fixture to all four corners of the ceiling. A scraggly bouquet of sunflowers, tied with tape, rested on the corner of a dual-sided partners' desk. Tim and Miz Vangie wore matching smiles, while Jim lounged against the wall with his arms folded across his chest. A short, balding man with a round face and a rounder belly stood behind the desk, holding an open book in his hands. "Come in. Come in," he said. "I'm Reverend Robson, and you must be the happy couple."

Eliza slipped her trembling hand into Mack's and he closed his fingers around it, thinking it felt right. He didn't know how he could feel good about anything at the moment, but her touch, her unspoken trust in him, felt wonderfully warm and appropriate. "What's this?" he said with a show of surprise. "Has a crime been committed in here?"

Laughter made the rounds, skipping only Deputy Jim.

"Now, don't be makin' jokes about crime in this office, Mack." Sheriff Tim stepped forward, all smiles and self-importance, to nudge Mack with his elbow. "Course, there are those that'd say matrimony is a crime."

The laughter made another incomplete circle. Everyone was certainly in a festive mood, Mack thought. Well, almost everyone. "Matrimony?" he said. "Is someone getting married?"

"You and Eliza." Miz Vangie's tone and demeanor took consent for granted as she approached him and pinned a single sunflower on his jumpsuit. "There. Now you look like a bridegroom."

"Miz Vangie thought it'd be fun to surprise you," the sheriff said. "This was mostly her idea."

Miz Vangie allowed herself a slight smile as she handed Eliza the sunflower bouquet. "It was the least I could do, after hittin' Mack like I did and then havin' him hauled off to jail."

"Really, there's no need to go to so much trouble," Mack said. "I knew all along it was just a misunderstanding." He turned to Sheriff Tim. "I'm not still under arrest, am I?"

"No, no." Tim grinned and shook his head. "Not now that Eliza explained how you and her came to be running loose in your—" he winked at Mack "—birthday suits."

Mack let that pass. "You know, this is all very thoughtful, but Eliza and I can't accept this—this..." Words failed him.

"But that's the whole idea." The sheriff dropped his arm, buddylike, around Mack's shoulder. "It's our way of saying, hey, we're sorry this happened to you on your weddin' day. I mean, after all the trouble you had to go to just to convince this little gal you wanted her to be your wife...well, we don't want you to have to wait another minute to be conjoined."

Eliza looked at Mack, wide-eyed and uncharacteristically silent. He squeezed her hand. "We appreciate your effort, but Eliza and I have some problems we have to work out before we can be...conjoined."

"Problems, pshaw!" Miz Vangie took Eliza's elbow in one hand and his elbow in the other and moved them into position before the Right Reverend Robson. "You get married first and that takes care of one big problem right off the bat."

"What problem?" Eliza asked.

"Lust," she replied.

Mack looked over his shoulder at the petite and strong-opinioned Miz Vangie. "But we have more than just, uh, that one problem to deal with and—"

"I know what your problem is, buster," she said with a decisive nod of her gray head. "Fear of commitment. Now, just stand there and do what the reverend tells ya and it'll all be over in a few minutes."

Mack upgraded the situation to serious as his gaze traveled from Miz Vangie's Mona Lisa smile to Reverend Robson's beaming face, connected briefly with Deputy Jim's suspicious frown and then moved on to the sheriff's bust-his-buttons grin. Very serious. Maybe Eliza was right and the truth had no place in this particular discussion. "This just isn't the place or the atmosphere Eliza and I had hoped to have for our wedding."

The atmosphere in the office grew slightly less festive as Deputy Jim uncrossed his arms and straightened away from the wall. "If I didn't know better, I'd say you sound downright ungrateful, MacKenzie."

There was a threat in there somewhere. Mack thought it might have been in the way his name had been pronounced—like Deputy Jim didn't entirely believe that *was* his name. "No," he said quickly. "No, that isn't true at all. It's just that..." he glanced at Eliza for inspiration " ...Eliza told me she's having second thoughts."

Miz Vangie pursed her wrinkled lips and stared him in the eye. "Any second thoughts she's havin' is because she's afraid you'll regret givin' up your inheritance in order to marry her. She needs to hear you say that money doesn't mean a thing to you and your life just isn't worth livin' without her."

Mack glanced at Sheriff Tim. "What if she really doesn't want to marry me?"

Tim looked at Eliza. "Well, do you?"

Eliza nodded, then seemed to rethink the question and started shaking her head.

"There," Miz Vangie said. "See, I told ya. She's just afraid you'll regret this."

He already regretted this, but Lord only knew what they'd do to him if he said so. "This is all so... unexpected."

"Unexpected?" A trace of his twin's suspicion crossed Sheriff Tim's face. "How can it be unexpected when you had to kidnap her right out from under the nose of that no-account bartender just before he could get her to say 'I do'?"

Mack turned his gaze on Eliza, who was beginning to look very pale and wan. "I thought you didn't tell them about him."

Reverend Robson cleared his throat. "Maybe we should allow the bride and groom a moment of privacy before the ceremony."

"They already had a moment," Deputy Jim said. "In the cell block. And they still aren't gettin' their stories straight. I say we either have this ceremony now or we hold them in jail until we can do a little more investigatin' into just who these two yahoos really are."

Miz Vangie faced the deputy with no more fear than an elephant has for a gnat. "Jim Cooper, I don't know why you're behavin' like a bear with a sore tooth, but I want you to stop it right now and join with us in helpin' these two young people celebrate their weddin'. Yahoos, indeed."

"But, Miz Vangie—"

"No buts, Jim. There is just no excuse for being inhospitable."

"Yeah." Tim stuck a camera in his brother's hands. "I'm the sheriff and I'm tellin' you to point and shoot that thing 'til I tell you to stop. Or until you run out of film, whichever happens first." He turned to cuff Mack on the shoulder. "Let's get this show on the road. Ready, Reverend?"

Mack couldn't think how to stop this runaway train, so he just stood there, holding Eliza's trembling hand and waiting to get run over.

"Dearly beloved," Reverend Robson began.

"Oh..." Eliza threw her arm across her forehead. "I think I'm going to faint!"

Mack gripped her elbow as she started to sag, but he saw her peeping at him and knew this was a tactical maneuver. "Oh, no, you don't," he said, inventing a tactical maneuver of his own. "You see, Miz Vangie? It isn't me who has the fear of commitment. It's Eliza. She doesn't want to marry me. She's still thinking about... him."

"That is pure nonsense!" The myopic gaze shifted from Eliza's flushed face to Mack's pained expression. "Now, if you just look at her and tell her you love her, then we can get on with the ceremony."

Eliza made a face, sighed and straightened in his arms. "All right, MacKenzie Cortland," she said. "I'm through trying to save you from disaster." She jerked the sunflowers into bridal-bouquet position, slipped her hand through the crook of his arm and faced the uncertain but still-smiling minister. "Reverend Robson? I do."

Chapter Ten

"Don't you think you've done enough already?" Mack asked.

"Now, now, there's no need to thank us." Sheriff Tim pushed open the door of Cabin 5 at the Hay Capitol Motel and stepped back. "Me and Jim wanted to do this. We thought you two deserved to spend what's left of your wedding night in a decent motel. We'll be back later in the mornin' to drive you down to Hutchinson and see about gettin' you a rental car."

"That's very kind," Mack said tightly. "But this is not necessary."

"Maybe not, but the room's paid for and you may as well put it to good use." Sheriff Cooper winked at Mack and nudged Eliza toward him. "Now, go on, son. Pick up your bride and carry her across the threshold."

Mack looked at her, and Eliza wished she could wipe out the frustration she saw in his eyes.

"Ready, Eliza?" Mack's voice lacked enthusiasm, and she tried to make her answer sound just as lackluster.

"Oh, absolutely," she said...and the next thing she knew he had scooped her roughly up in his arms. She barely got her hands around his neck before he was striding into the motel room with all the eagerness of a farmer on his way to clean out the chicken house. "Thanks, Sheriff Tim and Deputy Jim," she called over his shoulder. "This was really very nice of you!"

Mack clipped the door with his foot, sending it slamming shut on her words and the two men outside. In two strides, he reached the bed and dropped her onto it. The whole bedstead squeaked and wobbled under her weight. She braced her arms on the mattress and watched uneasily as Mack stepped back and looked around, his gaze ticking off the non-amenities of the Hay Capitol Motel.

"Hmm," he said. "How many stars do you suppose this place rates in the hotel guide?"

"I doubt it's listed."

"Really?" His critical gaze swung back to her. "Now, how could an oversight like that happen?"

"There's no reason to be hateful, Mack. This isn't exactly where I wanted to spend my honeymoon, either."

"Don't you mean *our* honeymoon?"

She flounced across the bed and bounced to her feet on the other side. "Look, it seemed like a good idea at the time. In fact, it seemed like the *only* idea at the time. If you had just let me faint, I might have been able to get us out of there unscathed."

He raised his eyebrows. "Unscathed? Did you say *unscathed?* Since I met you—an unbelievably long twelve hours ago—I have been kidnapped, robbed, stripped of my clothes and my dignity, punched, pinched, shot, bitten, whapped with a frying pan and thrown in jail for indecent exposure. That is not exactly a fair definition of unscathed."

"This hasn't exactly been a picnic for me, either."

"Oh, right, I forgot. You did get scared by that cow."

"*And* married. Don't forget that."

He massaged his forehead. "I'm likely to remember for the rest of my life."

"Well, I should hope so. You should be glad to have something like this to tell your grandchildren someday. I certainly am."

His hand slid to rub his jaw as he stared at her, taking in the saucy way her hair curled over her shoulder, the crimped, unflattering fit of the pink shirtwaist that couldn't quite conceal the full, lovely shape of her body, the spark of optimism in her wide gray eyes, the I-dare-you-to-make-a-mountain-out-of-a-molehill tilt of her chin. She had caused him untold trouble tonight, but just looking at her made him feel like a damn hero.

But then, he was an idiot. "Why would you ever tell anyone about that sham of a ceremony?"

One delicately curved eyebrow rose to challenge him. "Why wouldn't I? It was a beautiful little wedding in its own funny way. I mean, think about it. How many people get to have decorations made out of yellow streamers with the words *Warning. Do Not Cross. Crime Scene.* on them? The bride wore pink, the groom was in jail-house orange. The flowers were sunflowers...which was in keeping with the color theme. Instead of wedding cake and champagne, the refreshments were coffee and day-old doughnuts. I know this is dumb, but I actually got a lump in my throat when Reverend Robson and Sheriff Tim harmonized singing, 'On Top of Old Smoky'."

"That was a magic moment."

The corners of her mouth tightened. "Fine. Be that way. I'm just trying to see the bright side of all this. And before you jump in with another round of cynical comments, just let me say that if I *had* wanted to marry you, I'd think our wedding was full of the most romantic, precious memories I could ever hope to have."

There wasn't much he could say to that, not without offending her... or agreeing with her. And he wasn't quite fool enough to do either. "Look, if you don't mind, I'd like to try and call Leanne again."

Eliza felt like he'd punched her in the stomach, but she concealed her reaction with an indifferent shrug. "Why would I mind?"

"I meant, I'd prefer to make this call with a little privacy."

"Oh..." She realized she was in the way. "Oh, of course. I'll just go in the, uh, bathroom."

He picked up the phone and didn't even thank her for her understanding. It would serve him right if she just sat on the bed and stared at him while he made the call, but that would be petty and pointless. So she walked into the bathroom, which was small enough to qualify as a closet with a toilet, a sink, a mirror and a shower stall crammed inside. Not exactly the honeymoon suite. Her spirits dropped like a lead balloon. She never should have made fun of train travel.

"That's right. This is a collect call from MacKenzie Cortland." Mack propped the phone receiver on his shoulder and pulled out the drawer of the bedside table. Empty, except for an outdated catalog. He closed the drawer and looked around for something with an address or area code on it. Nothing. He didn't even know what town he was in. Cabin 5 of the Hay Capitol Motel in Sheridan County, Kansas, seemed to be the extent of his information, and he hoped it would be sufficient. On the other end of the line, he heard the phone ring once, then again, and he framed the opening words of his apology.

"Hello?" It was Leanne's voice, alert and curt.

"Leanne," he began, only to be interrupted by the operator.

"Collect call from MacKenzie Cortland. Will you accept the charges?"

There was a moment of silence and then Leanne said, "Never heard of him." And she hung up.

"I'm sorry, sir," the operator said. "She wouldn't accept the call."

"Try again, please." He glanced toward the bathroom, where he could see Eliza's reflection in the mirror. She was leaning against the wall, her arms crossed, her head bent, her dark hair falling seductively forward on either side of her face. She looked pale and unhappy, and he was ashamed of himself for blaming her for everything. Just because she hadn't handled the situation the way he thought she should have didn't mean he was exempt from responsibility. Much as he hated to admit it, most of the burden of failure belonged to him. He could have made better choices. Would have, no doubt, if his head hadn't been pounding like a sledgehammer. Still, he couldn't believe he'd actually stood there and said "I do." Wouldn't jail have been preferable? What had he been thinking? And how was he going to—

"I'm sorry, sir." The operator's voice intruded on his thoughts. "No one is answering."

He sighed and wished Leanne wasn't so inflexible. "Please, try one more time, and let it ring as long as you can."

Eliza lifted her head, and her gaze met his in the mirror. She looked startled to find him watching her, but then, almost as if she had no control over it, a tentative smile tipped the corners of her mouth . . . a smile that offered encouragement, support and simple respect. And with that shy, hesitant and unexpected response, his frustration slowly abated. As bad as this night had been, he couldn't regret it, not when Eliza was so determined to make the best of the situation. Not when he thought about how glad he was, at this particular moment, not to be on a train to Miami.

He moved his head, silently asking Eliza to join him. She looked confused, and he raised his hand to motion for her to come out of the bathroom. She wrinkled her nose in indecision. He raised his shoulders in an exaggerated shrug. She pursed her lips. He made a face. And then she came out of seclusion.

"Sir?" The operator returned. "I'm sorry, but I don't believe anyone is going to answer."

He nodded. "Thank you for trying." He hung up. "She won't take the call."

"Did she know it was you?"

He leaned back against the headboard. "I'm pretty certain that's why she won't take the call."

"I don't understand. If I were in her place, I'd be so glad just to hear from you."

That odd tightness in his chest returned. "Would you, Eliza? Even if I'd ruined the most important day of your life?"

"Don't be silly. What could be more important than knowing you're all right?" She plopped down on the bed beside him. "Try again. She must have been asleep or something and not understood the call was from you."

He looked at her generous, persuasive smile and wondered what it would be like to fall in love with someone who believed so completely, so compellingly, that there was good in every situation and that there was at least one redeeming quality in every person.

"Here, I'll do it." She leaned across him, reaching for the phone and sending a shock of awareness through him as her breasts brushed innocently, but oh, so tantalizingly, across his chest. "What's her number?"

His eyebrows shot up and he tried to adjust his position on the bed so he could withdraw from temptation without attracting undo attention. "You can't call Leanne."

"Why not? She won't talk to you."

"No, and she isn't going to talk to you, either." He plumped a lumpy pillow and stuffed it between his back and the headboard, taking care to keep his chest separated from Eliza's by at least a quarter of an inch or so. "Call your family, instead, and let them know you're all right."

She shrugged off the suggestion. "There's only Auntie Gem, and it's too late to call her. I'd only scare her to death. Come on, tell me the number. I'll bet I can get Leanne to talk to you."

"Trust me, Eliza. Drop it."

"Are you sure? I'm a pretty good persuader."

If she were half as good at persuading as she was at explanations, he figured she could fix it so Leanne would never speak to him again. Come to think of it, maybe he should let her call. "It doesn't matter if you do get her to answer. She's not going to listen to anything I have to say tonight."

Eliza's dark eyes flashed doubt, and Mack decided he was getting out of the Pollyanna-protector business. "All right," he said and told her the number. "You'll need to call collect. I don't think Sheriff Tim thought we'd be needing any long-distance credit on our motel tab."

"Don't worry." She punched in a long series of numbers. "I have a phone card. I knew someday I'd be glad I memorized the number. Ssh, it's ringing."

She leaned back against the headboard beside him and held the receiver away from her ear so he could hear that it was, indeed, ringing. He shrugged, settled back and waited to say he'd told her so.

"Operator, I told you I don't know this man. Now stop annoying me with these phone calls!" Leanne's voice blasted out of the receiver, and Mack sat up so fast he bumped his head on the wall sconce that hung directly over the bed.

"Leanne?" Eliza said, happily giving him a thumbs-up sign as she clapped the receiver against her ear. "Hi. This isn't the operator. This is Eliza. Eliza Richards... we met on the church steps today? I knew you'd be concerned about Mack, and I just wanted you to know that he's fine. He's had kind of a rough night, but he's feeling much better and there's nothing for you to worry about. Well, no, of course you don't have to worry if you don't... Look, just talk to him for a minute. Here....." She thrust the phone receiver at Mack.

He took it and held it as if it were a live grenade. "Leanne?" he said cautiously.

"Who is that?" she demanded, without a nuance of concern in her clipped, accusing tones.

He frowned. "Eliza?"

"I know her name, Mack. I want to know where you are and what she is doing there with you."

He first felt anger at her accusatory tone and then a slowly building resentment that she had so little respect for his character. "I'm at the Hay Capitol Motel," he said distinctly. "And at this precise moment, Eliza and I are sharing a bed."

"You son of a bitch. Isn't it bad enough that you humiliated me and disgraced your family by running away with that woman? Did you have to call and make certain I'm suffering because of your betrayal?"

He clenched his fist around the phone receiver. "I did not betray you, Leanne."

"Oh, right," she said in that awful nasal voice she used whenever she wanted to put someone in his place. "I am not stupid, Mack. I saw the way you looked at her. And I will never—"

"I was kidnapped," he cut in tersely.

"—forgive you," she continued without a break. "Do you understand? Never! You've made your bed, so lie in it and leave me alone!"

The phone hummed in his ear and he stared at the receiver, conscious only of the wish that he'd been quick enough to hang up on her first. He tossed the receiver toward its cradle and didn't much care when it clattered across the table and fell to the floor. "I think I liked it better when she wasn't answering."

Eliza scooped the hair up off her nape and pushed it into a dark, disheveled cluster on top of her head. "I guess she was a little upset, huh?"

He shrugged. "A little. She didn't buy the kidnapping story."

Eliza released her hair and it fell in a dusky cloud about her shoulders. "Are you surprised?"

"Not especially. Leanne is not a particularly good listener."

"After that crack about the motel and sharing the bed with me, I can't say I blame her. Honestly, Mack, what possessed you to say such a thing?"

"Gee, Eliza, I don't know." He yanked the pillow from behind his back and pumped some air into it with a few quick jabs. "Maybe I'm just not as good a 'persuader' as you."

"Now, look, it isn't my fault she wouldn't listen."

He glanced at her, then plopped the pillow at the head of the bed and slid down so his head fell on it. "No, how could that be your fault?" Settling his hands behind his head, he stared, frustrated and angry, at the ceiling. "And even if I could prove it was, I am not stupid enough to get into that kind of argument with you now."

The bed jiggled as she twisted around to look at him. "Why not now? You brought it up."

"Not now, Eliza, because *now* is almost two in the morning. It has been a very long night and I intend to take Leanne's advice and lie in the bed I made for myself. I suggest you do the same."

"What are you saying? That I should lie in this bed with you?"

"As there's only this one bed, that would seem logical."

"Logical? You think sharing a bed is logical?"

"Yes, I do."

"Well, that doesn't make much sense."

"I don't see why not. We are married and married people generally share a bed."

"We are not married and you know it. That ceremony, even if it was legal, was not real."

He closed his eyes against the dull pain in his head . . . or was it his heart that was hurting? "It was real, Eliza, and it was legal. What did you think you were signing when the sheriff shoved that license in front of you?"

"Your release papers? I don't know. I didn't really think about it. It seemed like the quickest, most-efficient way of getting you out of jail."

"And now you're having second thoughts and wishing you'd left me to rot in that cell." The bed jiggled again and he felt her gaze on him.

"No," she said. "I'd do it all over again if I thought it was necessary. All I'm saying is that you didn't make a true commitment to me and you're not bound by anything you said during the ceremony, and it's really not in your best interest to sleep with me."

"Really? What's going to happen to me? A knee in the kidneys? A fist in the face? A foot in the backside?"

"Leanne is going to kill you."

"Not until I've had at least a couple of hours sleep."

"That isn't the point, Mack."

He opened his eyes and looked at her, all solemn and earnest and appealing. "Eliza, I am going to lie here and try my best to fall asleep. And it would be in your best interest to do the same."

"I can't sleep. Not now."

"Okay, lie there and stare at the ceiling."

"I can't do that, either. Then I'll just worry about you and Leanne and Mrs. Pageatt and the police and Chuck and the million-dollar dress. You know, I really should be out looking for it right now."

"No, you shouldn't. Please lie down and rest a little."

"No. I've got to straighten out this mess."

His sigh was long and patient. "Eliza, could we just keep life simple for a little while? No explanations, no worrying about what needs to happens next. Just a couple of hours of no-fault sleep?"

"I'm sorry, Mack, but I cannot sleep with you."

"How about beside me?"

She frowned down at him and shook her head, as if he were dense. "It will just complicate everything. Don't you understand? If you have any hope of straightening out your relationship with Leanne, then one of us has to leave. Now."

"I have no hope. I have only a headache."

"But you see what I'm saying, don't you?"

He pushed up and braced his weight on his elbows. "Would it help if I strung a blanket down the middle of the bed?"

She shook her head. "I saw that movie, and Clark Gable only got away with it because there were twin beds in the room. Besides, it wouldn't matter. I don't think Leanne will believe that we stayed in the same cabin and just slept, even if we were in separate beds."

"Eliza, in the past several hours, we've been stripped naked and tied back-to-back. We've tumbled around a haystack in our birthday suits and stumbled into the farmyard of Annie Oakley without a stitch to call our own. Do you honestly think it matters if we sleep in the same bed?''

"It will matter to your fiancée."

"I don't have a fiancée. I have a wife. Now, let's get some sleep, shall we?"

"I'll sleep in the bathroom, then."

"No, you won't." He grabbed her hand before she could bounce her way off the bed. With a single tug, he pulled her off balance and she toppled down beside him, warm, sweet-smelling and vulnerable. "I'm sure you would stand in that bathroom until daybreak just so you could honestly say that we didn't sleep together. But that isn't necessary and it isn't going to happen. I promise never to reveal to another living soul what happens in this bed if you'll just stay here and get some rest. Now, can you live with that kind of compromise?"

"Can I sleep on top of the covers?"

He had never met anyone like her. "If you're comfortable, I'm comfortable."

"But one of us should probably sleep under the covers."

"Your choice."

"Okay, I'm fine on top."

"Good, so am I."

"But we're both—"

"Eliza, do me a favor?"

"What?"

"Stop talking."

The memory of how he'd stopped her before filled the room. "Oh," she said with breathy awareness. "I'll just scoot down here and try to go to sleep."

He half wished she'd put up more of a fight. "Good idea," he said and slid down beside her.

ELIZA AWAKENED at one point, shivering and cold. Dawn sliced through a gap in the drapes and cast an eerie glow across the motel room. It took several minutes before the memory of where she was and why filtered through the haze of sleep to find her, but oddly, she wasn't startled by the strange surroundings or the soft, reassuring sounds of Mack's breathing.

Carefully, so as not to disturb him, she rolled over until they lay face to sleeping face and she could look at him as much and as long as she wished. He didn't look like the man she'd always pictured as her soul mate. She didn't know how, exactly, but she'd imagined her bridegroom would look different, somehow. It was too bad she couldn't recall the details of the man she'd seen in the mirror. Maybe he'd looked like Mack, although she really couldn't be sure.

Her lips curved with a tender smile. Why was she thinking about a man who probably didn't even exist when she was lying next to Mack? She wanted to spend what time she had drowning in the delicious sensations she felt just looking at him. He wasn't handsome, exactly. His face was too angular for that. But his features were strong and appealing. And she liked his hair as it was now, mussed and relaxed, with a few dark strands falling like shadows across his forehead. In sleep, he lost the precise, proper look of a man of purpose and became approachable, touchable and oh, so desirable.

MacKenzie Cortland. Even his name pleased her, and she tried it on for size. Mrs. MacKenzie Cortland. Eliza Cortland. Not that she would ever use it, of course. Or ever speak it aloud. Or even whisper it in private. But here, in the dusky, dusty confines of Cabin 5, she allowed herself to pretend—just for a moment—that MacKenzie Cortland belonged, in name and body, to her.

She lifted her hand and came within a breath of stroking his cheek with her fingertip. But what would she say if she awakened him? How could she tell him she'd just wanted to know what it felt like to touch him, her husband, in the first, sweet moments of dawn? And how could she possibly explain that she had been so reckless and foolish as to fall in love with a man who rightfully belonged to another?

THE MOMENT HE OPENED his eyes and saw Eliza watching him, Mack knew he was in trouble. There wasn't time for her to mask her expression, and he recognized it for what it was...a wishful, wistful longing. A desire born of needs he knew nothing of, but understood very well. Without a second's consideration, he surrendered to impulse and reached for her, pulling her into his arms and into an embrace he suddenly wanted more than anything else. He moved his head on the pillow and felt her warm breath on his face an instant before he pressed his mouth to hers.

Passion awakened in him, fierce and pulsing, as if it had lain too long asleep, and he kissed her with ruthless possession. Her response fed his hunger, greedily taking pleasure from his touch and demanding more. Her body sought the curve of his and nestled against him in seductive petition. Her silky skin stroked his neck as her arms slid around him, drawing him closer...closer....

He kissed her long and thoroughly, taking the time to learn the shape of her lips, the taste of her skin, the untouched yearning of her generous heart. His fingers worked the buttons of her dress, freeing the ma-

terial so he could push it back and reach the tender
pulse points beneath. He kissed her throat, her neck,
the soft hollow of her shoulder, and returned to her
lips to begin again, imprinting the feel of her in his
mind, memorizing the details that made up the one-
and-only Eliza.

Another button slipped free, inviting him to explore the smoothness of her breastbone, the gentle
slopes of her body, the lusty fullness of her breasts.
She wore a nylon slip beneath the dress, but no bra.
Miz Vangie's wardrobe obviously had its limitations,
he thought, as his hand slipped between the crisp cotton dress fabric and the slick, sheer synthetic. Eliza
caught her breath in a quicksilver gasp as his hand
closed over her breast.

He looked at her, searching for her thoughts, her
feelings, her desire to stop... or proceed. The expression in her eyes was cloudy with excitement, and he
didn't wait for further invitation before he trailed a
line of kisses down the open V and dampened the thin
nylon with several enticing strokes of his tongue. He
grew tired of being separated from her by even such a
thin layer of clothing, and in a moment, he moved his
hand to impatiently pull the strap off her shoulder and
release the swell of her breast. Her fingers pushed beneath the collar of his jumpsuit and dug lightly into his
shoulders as he drew her into his mouth. His suckling
drew a quiet, nearly inaudible cry of pleasure from her
lips, and the sound wounded him with its honesty.

Simultaneously, he felt a contradictive rush of protective emotion and physical desire. He wanted to
protect her and possess her, to explore her mystery and
to respect her secrets. But he couldn't resist the temptation to continue touching, kissing, giving pleasure

and taking pleasure in the giving. Eliza was so easy to please, so eager to respond. And he wondered how he had lived all his life without realizing how unpredictable and sweet life could be.

He knew the moment she became aware of just where they were heading. He recognized the subtle shift of her attention from the physical to the practical. He could feel the tension as it skimmed across her body in a nearly indiscernible ripple. For the space of a heartbeat or two, he thought about sabotaging her doubt with a rush of new sensations, with dozens of soul-devouring kisses that would once more shift the balance of reason and passion. But he had never taken anything that wasn't his, and married or not, Eliza did not belong to him.

With more regret than he cared to admit, he rolled onto his back and stared at the ceiling, unsettled by the tension in his own body, caught lonely and needy by the sharp protest of his heart. If he'd gone on, if he'd pressed for intimacy, would she have denied him? Would he have used the excuse of the ceremony to seduce her? Would she have pretended to believe the marriage was for real? And if she hadn't, would he have had the sense to stop on his own? Eliza was right about avoiding further complications. She was completely right and he... He was awash in desire.

"Mack." Her voice was a thoughtful whisper beside him. "You kissed me."

He frowned at the ceiling. "Yes."

Silence ticked like a clock, measuring the questions huddled in the bed between them. "You kissed me," she repeated in a hushed and wondering voice. "And I wasn't even talking. There was no excuse for it."

"No," he agreed, confirming the suspicion that she couldn't quite put into words. "There was no excuse for it at all. Except that I wanted to kiss you."

She sighed and rolled onto her back beside him. For several long minutes, they each stared overhead. "Mack," she said finally. "I wanted to kiss you, too."

I know, Eliza. He didn't answer her aloud, though. He couldn't say anything else without putting them both in danger. So he lay, focusing on the ceiling and wondering why doing the right thing had suddenly become so frustrating.

Chapter Eleven

Water spewed from the shower head in a lukewarm drizzle, unaffected by Mack's efforts to adjust the pressure and temperature. He twisted the knobs again in frustration and decided that even the showers in this place were conservative—not too hot, not too cold. Normally that would have suited him fine, but he'd been counting on a cold shower to shock some sense into him. Not to mention shocking some of the foolishness out of him. He couldn't believe after everything that had happened to him yesterday how his body went into red alert just lying in bed next to Eliza. How could he be attracted to her? He barely knew her. Amazing.

And he was married to her. Even more amazing. He stuck his head under the low-pressure stream and let the water wash over him. Cortlands must be turning in their mausoleums all across the country. The family history was liberally seasoned with long engagements that inevitably led to long marriages. Divorce didn't occur in the Cortland dynasty, because the men chose their brides the same way they chose their suits...with deliberate attention to quality, style and the proper fit.

He considered Eliza and decided that he had already seen evidence of courage, resolve, ingenuity and a sense of humor—all qualities he admired. And as to style...well, any woman who could carry off wearing such dissimilar raiment as a bridal gown, her birthday suit, a prim flannel nightgown and a 1950s shirtwaist with saddle shoes didn't have much to fear when it came to fashion. But proper fit was something else entirely...and there was no way in heaven or hell that Eliza Richards would ever fit into the staid, sedate and ultraorthodox Cortland family. And he wouldn't want her if she did.

He filled his hands with the lukewarm water and splashed it on his face, shaking his head to sling away the excess moisture. There wasn't even any reason for him to be thinking about it. As she had been quick to point out, the marriage might be legal, but it wasn't real and could be annulled without fault on either side. And there was no question that it should be. So why was he plagued by a persistent and mutinous desire to consummate this strange union with Eliza and spend the day—maybe several days—making long, passionate love to her?

He tried again to regulate the temperature, but no matter which way he turned the taps, the spray remained unchanged. Maybe that doctor had been wrong and he actually did have a concussion. It was possible that his muddled reasoning this morning was a direct result of the bump on his head. Anyone who'd been knocked unconscious by a frying pan—make that anyone who'd been hit with a frying pan and then used as a battering ram—had a legitimate excuse for behaving as if he had mincemeat for brains. And his body had suffered significant trauma during this little adventure... which, come to think of it, didn't do anything to explain his sexual "pertness" this morning.

But no matter. He hadn't spent the past thirty-four years as a Cortland without learning to control himself, his emotions and his circumstances. And this would be no different. Eliza was an earthquake in the otherwise-serene landscape of his life, and from this moment on, he would treat her as such. He'd phone Leanne again after he got out of the shower. He'd say whatever he had to say, promise whatever he had to promise, to persuade her that he was an innocent bystander in the crazy events that had made a shambles of their wedding day. And eventually she'd believe him—or pretend to, anyway. And his life would go back to the way it had been before Eliza had rumbled through it.

A draft of air whisked past him suddenly and he looked around, fully expecting to see a gap in the wall joists or a crack in the window above the shower stall, but everything looked solid and sta—

The plastic shower curtain made a popping sound and billowed toward him. Startled, he jerked back, slipped and grabbed for support, catching the hot-water knob in both hands and barely preventing a fall.

"Mack?"

"Eliza—!" Hot water gushed from the shower head in a sudden burst, and he scrambled out of the stall, nearly falling over her in his haste to avoid being broiled.

Eliza grasped his forearm to steady him as an ocean of steam poured into the tiny bathroom. "What happened?" she asked in alarm. "Are you all right?"

He looked down at the not-so-supple plastic curtain that was plastered across him from shoulder to hip and somehow wasn't surprised when it began a slow slide off his slick body. "Couldn't you have just knocked on the door like a normal person?"

Her chin came up and she dropped her hand from his arm. "I did knock. You obviously didn't hear me."

"Right." He was rather pleased with the succinct syllable and the way it snicked through the humid, heated air. "And of course, you couldn't have waited two more minutes for me to finish my shower, could you, Miss Impulsive?"

Her eyes sparked in anger and she shoved a towel into his hand. "That's *Mrs.* Impulsive to you." She spun on her heel, nicking his big toe with the clunky sole of her borrowed saddle oxford as she left the bathroom and closed the door decisively behind her.

Hell, Mack thought, as he reached around and shut off the waterfall behind him. Now what was wrong with her? It wasn't lack of sleep, that was for sure. She had gotten plenty of shut-eye. Certainly more than he had. She hadn't lain awake trying to convince herself she wasn't really attracted to him. She hadn't watched him sleep or memorized every part of his face or counted the number of times he'd sighed in peaceful dreams. Oh, no, she'd slept like a baby, leaving him to deal with a strange bevy of unexpectedly tender and absolutely inappropriate emotions.

Damn it, he had a right to be irritable. A healthy annoyance was probably the best thing for him...probably his only real means of defense, as well. Eliza looked rested and pretty this morning. A single smile from her might send his resolve packing. A thread of her laughter could trip up his best intentions. She was impulsive and unpredictable and, for God only knew what reason, he found her profoundly seductive.

Why had she come into the bathroom, anyway? To stir him up? Get his blood pumping? Raise his body temperature? He pressed his fingers into a wad of soft terry cloth. Had she come in just to bring him a towel? He winced, realizing he'd overreacted to her completely innocent and thoughtful gesture.

Sighing in frustration, he rubbed the terry cloth over his wet hair and wiped his face. Then, looping the towel behind his back, he made several passes across his shoulders before dropping it to his hips and doing a little rumba. He then brought it around to wipe his chest and legs before dropping it and reaching for his coveralls. The moment he stepped into the jumpsuit, the material clamped around his ankle with a cool, clammy wetness. Water from the runaway shower had collected on the floor, forming a puddle right where he'd dropped his clothes before stepping into the shower. The jumpsuit was soaked from the thighs down and all along one side from neck to sleeve.

What was he supposed to do now? Hang them out the window? And then what? Stay in the bathroom until they dried? On the other hand, parading around the motel room in his jail-house-issue boxers was not a particularly attractive option, either. Tough choice. Make that no choice.

Reaching down, he picked up the boxers with his thumb and forefinger and held them up while they dripped like a leaky faucet onto his bare feet. He let go and the underwear dropped with a splash on the floor. And he'd had such hopes for this morning, too. Retrieving the damp towel, he wrapped its abbreviated length about his waist and opened the door. "Eliza? Could you... give me a hand?"

She stopped leafing through the outdated catalog to look at him. Sitting in the middle of the bed, her legs criss-crossed beneath the pouf of the pink skirt, she looked like a pale pink tulip sprouting from the center of the sea-foam green cotton sheets. With a slight and maddening smile, she brought up her hands and gave him a round of applause.

"Very funny. Come on, Eliza. I need some assistance here. My clothes were on the bathroom floor and they got a little...damp. Do you think you could find something for me to wear?"

She held up the catalog. "This might work for you." She tapped the picture of a trench coat. "With some black socks and shoes? What do you think?"

"Very classy, but I had something a little more immediate in mind."

"I'm pretty sure they'll deliver."

"They'll deliver me straight to jail in that outfit, with or without Miz Vangie's frying pan. Come on, now, give me a—" He held up his hand, his palm out. "Help me find something to wear. Please?"

Tilting her head to the side, she looked him over from toe to towel, adding a hot flash of awareness to his already overheated irritation. "Scrawny towel, isn't it?"

"It's adequate."

She shook her head and sighed. "If I had a couple of safety pins, I could fix you a bedspread toga. But I have to be honest with you, Mack. I don't think it would be very flattering."

His lips tightened. "You wouldn't be enjoying this so much if you were the one without anything to wear."

"You know, you're right." She began to hum softly as she resumed leafing through the catalog.

He couldn't believe it, she was humming. "Fine. I'll take care of this myself." He walked toward the bed and was gratified to see a glint of wariness in her eyes. Ignoring her for the moment, he picked up the phone from the floor and set it on the bedside table. He dialed zero and waited for someone in the motel office to answer.

Eliza felt his eyes on her and nonchalantly turned a page in the catalog. All right, so adding to his irritation was probably not the wisest course she could have chosen this morning, she thought. But then, he hadn't taken any pains to put her at ease, either. Impulsive, he'd said. As if it was something to be ashamed of. As if she was responsible for everything that had happened. As if she had completely ruined his life.

Even if most of what had happened *was* her fault, he didn't have to keep pointing it out. As if she didn't know what a tangle they were in. They? Make that what a tangle *she* was in. Mack was going to walk out of this cabin a free man. He'd have to get the marriage annulled, of course, but she couldn't see that as being much of a problem. It had only taken a few misunderstandings and a couple of signatures to do the deed. How could it take more than a statement of the truth and a signature to undo it? In fact, when all was said and done, she'd probably be lucky if he didn't sue her for impersonating his wife or some such thing. And if he didn't think of suing her, his fiancée undoubtedly would.

She sighed. His fiancée. Avoiding the use of her name wasn't going to do any good. Leanne wasn't going to disappear from Mack's life just because Eliza had been silly enough to go and fall in love with him. And to think she'd stood in that jail and *married* him! Of all the dim-witted, foolhardy, impulsive things she'd done in her lifetime, that had to take the cake— or doughnut.

Stop it, she thought. *Don't think about the doughnuts, the sunflowers or the "I do's."* The ceremony wasn't any more real than any of the weddings she'd ever imagined for herself. And Mack was completely justified in being upset with her this morning. She had *impulsively* involved him in her problems, and all he had done was try gallantly to rescue her. The least she could do was to be on her best behavior for whatever brief amount of time they still had together.

"No answer." He dropped the phone receiver in frustration. "Apparently no one's in the office."

"The motel office?"

"Where else would you call for room service?"

Best behavior. She silently repeated her resolve as she met his exasperated gaze. "I could have told you he wasn't there."

"Who?"

"Ken Cooper," she said politely. "Sheriff and Deputy Cooper's cousin. He owns this motel."

"How do you know that?"

"Well, because he was just here, and we got to talking and he told me."

"He was just here? You mean while I was in the shower?"

She nodded, under control, but annoyed by the edge of sarcasm in his voice. "He brought some towels, because he wasn't sure we had enough, since we checked in so late. And besides, he wanted to let us know that we get a complimentary breakfast at the Sunflower Café across the street." She smiled, hoping the thought of free food would go a long way toward soothing his inexplicable tension.

Instead, he cinched the knot of his towel with an agitated tug. "You interrupted my shower and nearly scalded me just to inform me that we get a damned complimentary breakfast?"

Control vanished. Aggravation won the day. "No, Mack, I interrupted your shower because he said he needed to talk to you as soon as possible and I *impulsively* thought you might want to know *as soon as possible.*"

"What does he want to talk to me about?"

"I didn't ask."

His lips tightened. "Oh, come on. You expect me to believe you didn't try to find out what he wanted so you could have the pleasure of explaining it to me?"

She flung the catalog to the floor and bounced off the jiggly bed. "I don't know what is wrong with you this morning, but I didn't get much sleep and I'm in no mood to—"

"Bull."

"I beg your pardon?"

"I said bull. You slept like a baby."

"How would you know? You slept like a log!"

"On the contrary, I dozed fitfully and spent the rest of the time watching you snooze."

"I don't think so, because *I* dozed fitfully and watched *you* snooze."

The knowledge that they had watched each other sleep, that in the early morning darkness they had taken turns at being awake and aware, seeped into the air like an enticing aroma. Mack's eyes met hers in a brief but telling exchange before he looked away.

"You slept at least three hours."

His accusation lacked fervor, as did her reply. "Well, you slept at least four, so there."

"Fine, have it your way. I got more sleep than you did. Is that what you wanted to hear?"

She pushed her hair back behind her ear. "I don't know what I wanted to hear or even why I said that, and I certainly don't understand why we're having this argument."

Mack lifted his gaze to hers again. The look in her eyes made her breathless for the space of a dozen heartbeats before he turned abruptly and paced to the window. "Don't you? Don't you even have a clue?"

Eliza didn't have much experience with men in the morning, but she sensed that this argument had less to do with lack of sleep than with a strained awareness, an elusive tension she was hesitant to analyze. "Well," she said, without any idea of what she ought to say. "If I have to guess, I'd say it's because I have something to wear and you don't."

He lifted the curtain and looked out the window. "No, Eliza. We're arguing because if we don't, I'm going to kiss you."

She couldn't breathe again, couldn't even think straight. "That would be a change," she said raspily. "Usually you kiss me because I am talking. Except for last night. Last night, I wasn't talking and you—"

"Eliza, this would be an excellent time for you to take a walk. I'd go myself, but I'm a little underdressed for a stroll."

"You want me to leave?"

He let go of the curtain, which swung shut over the window as he turned to look at her. "No, I don't want you to leave. I *want* to make love to you, but since that is completely out of the question, I would appreciate a little time alone to get my errant emotions under control. Is that explanation clear enough for you?"

The thrill of discovery sent a tingle skating down her spine. "You're attracted to me?" she whispered. "Really?"

He rubbed the back of his neck, while the corners of his mouth formed a melancholy curve. "Eliza, if I didn't know it was impossible, I'd be tempted to believe I'm half in love with you. Those are the kind of mind games I'm facing this morning so, yes, I am desperately attracted to you, and you should get the hell out of this cabin before I do something we'll both regret."

Her heart stopped dead in its tracks and enfolded his words for safe keeping before resuming its runaway pace. "Only half..." she said in a thin, reedy voice, playing the possibility over and over in her mind. "Which isn't anything like completely. But still, it's nice of you to tell me. Even though it's impossible that you...that we...well, of course, you couldn't just forget about Leanne. I can't just forget about her, either. Even if we are married. Even if I wouldn't regret..." Her words trailed into a tense silence, and she knew if she looked at him, saw the faintest hint of desire in his eyes...

"You're right, Mack, I should just go on over to the café." She edged toward the door, fighting the impulse to stay with every step. "I'll just get out of here. Get out of your way for a while. Maybe I'll go get some coffee or breakfast or something...."

He stayed where he was, watching her movements, stalking her with a hungry stare, tempting her to forget every principle in favor of a worthless piece of paper. She felt the doorknob at her back and reached behind her to clasp its cool reality. Swallowing hard, she turned the knob. "I read somewhere that a cold shower...?"

"I already tried that."

She pulled the knob and stepped back into the opening. "I meant...actually, I was thinking more in terms of... well, I wondered if maybe I should try a cold shower myself."

He closed his eyes. "Go, Eliza."

She went.

"MACK?" Eliza pushed open the cabin door. "I brought you some breakfast."

Silence greeted her announcement and, frowning, she carefully backed into the room, trying to keep the screen door from smashing into the plastic box and cups in her hands. Once safely inside, she placed the food on the table and walked over to the bathroom. It wasn't big enough for a hiding place, and she couldn't imagine that he'd try to hide from her, anyway. Unless he thought she might have spent the last hour plotting ways to take advantage of him. The thought swirled pleasurably inside her. And if he'd been here—which he clearly wasn't—maybe she would have. But he wasn't here. Maybe he'd decided to remove himself from the temptation of being in the same room, seeing her and wanting her and—

She put the brakes on her rambunctious imagination, opened one of the cups and sipped the coffee. She had spent nearly an hour in the Sunflower Café, getting acquainted with Arnetta, the waitress, and her nephew, Tom, who had stopped by on his way to Topeka. She'd chatted briefly with Ken Cooper, who'd come into the café to get "caffeine on the hoof," which turned out to be a diet cola. She'd asked him about borrowing some clothes for Mack and listened while he related a long, involved story about the first time he'd gone backpacking in Colorado. She'd eaten a hearty breakfast and ordered one to go. And the whole time, all she could think about was Mack's words, *I'm half in love with you. I'm half in love with you. I'm half in love with you.*

She wandered over to the bed and smoothed the rumpled covers. He'd watched her sleep. The thought was sweetly provocative, and on impulse, she reached down and rumpled the covers again. She liked it better that way. Picking the catalog up off the floor, she dropped it on the bedside table and then opened the curtains. Sunlight spilled in, making the cabin bright, cozy and rustically charming. What a great place to spend a honeymoon, she thought. If, of course, it was possible to meet the man of your dreams, marry him and go on a honeymoon all in the span of one night. She drank the coffee as the sunshine warmed her from the inside out. Mack might spend the rest of his life denying it could happen, but she'd spend the rest of hers knowing it could.

He found her attractive. He had wanted to make love to her. He was half in love with her. And she was impulsively, foolishly and totally in love with him. The emotion sang in her heart like a songbird, wrapping her in delicious possibilities.

On a whim, she unlatched the window and raised it, letting the clean morning air circulate into the room.

What a great place, she thought. Just the fact that the windows weren't nailed shut seemed like an omen of a bright future ahead. Why, she wouldn't be surprised if—

Crunching gravel and voices caught her attention. She poked her head out the window, trying to see who was approaching the cabin. Although the angle of the window prevented her from seeing, as the footsteps got closer, she easily identified Mack's voice.

"—Rather you let me handle Eliza, Sheriff Cooper. She spooks easily, and if I can have just a few minutes alone with her, I think I can explain what's happened without panicking her."

"I understand completely." The sheriff's voice faded as if he'd changed directions, and Eliza leaned farther out the window, trying to catch what he was saying. "—Just unfortunate, and there's no reason to upset her any more than necessary. I don't know why Jim got it into his head to call the KCPD—that's short for Kansas City Police Department, in case you didn't know—in the first place. But he's like that sometimes, 'specially when he gets to thinking somethin' isn't just the way it oughta be, and then he's bound and determined to get to the bottom of it and I can't talk no sense into him nohow, no way."

"I'm sure this can all be cleared up with a couple of phone calls," Mack said. "To be honest, I'm surprised Leanne even reported this as a suspected kidnapping."

"Yeah, well, you know what they say about hell and a woman scorned."

"I do know. That's why I'm surprised."

Eliza heard the squeak as the screen door opened, and she hastily pulled back inside, turning quickly to brace herself and lean casually on the sill. She sheathed her racing thoughts with an expression of easy good humor and hoped her panic was adequately concealed. "Hi," she said the moment the door swung open. "I brought you some breakfast."

Mack paused with his hand on the knob. He was wearing a pair of tight-fitting jeans and a denim shirt with the sleeves rolled to his elbows. His boots were the same ones from last night, but he was freshly shaved and terribly attractive. Her heart ached just at the sight of him, and she knew she'd been a fool not to stay, not to take advantage when she'd had the chance. His gaze traveled from her to the open window at her back to her nonchalant pose to the plastic containers on the table before he stepped inside and firmly closed the door.

"Hi," he said. "Thanks, I can use something to eat."

"No problem. I see you got some dry clothes. Did Ken bring them? I saw him at the café and mentioned that you'd tried to call the office to borrow some. You might want to eat that." She indicated the food with a nod. "I figured you were hungry enough to eat just about anything, and that's what I told Arnetta. She's the waitress at the Sunflower, in case you were wondering, and I also met this guy who offered to give me a ride as far as Topeka, but I—"

"Eliza." Mack silenced her with a look. "How much did you overhear?"

She feigned surprise. "Overhear? When?"

"Just now, that's when."

"I don't know what you're talking about."

"Give it up, Eliza." He walked to the edge of the bed and looked at her across the rumpled covers. "The window's open, and knowing you as well as I do, I'm certain that a moment ago you were hanging over that sill, eavesdropping on my conversation with the sheriff."

She lifted her chin. "You hardly know me at all."

"Don't bet on that."

He kept further protests at bay with an arrogant arch of his brow, and if she hadn't been preoccupied with what she'd overheard, she'd have called his bluff.

"Now," he continued. "Let me explain what has happened and what we're going to do about it." He moved to the table and uncapped the lid on the coffee cup. "Leanne seems to have come to the belated realization that I was forced to leave the wedding." He paused and looked at the cup in his hand. "Imagine my surprise. She actually believed me last night when I said I was kidnapped. After she'd hung up, of course, but still..." He shrugged, drank some of the coffee, then set the cup on the table. "So, upon realizing that one, I might be in actual danger, and that two, having her bridegroom kidnapped was preferable to being jilted, she contacted the KCPD—that's short for the Kansas City Police Department, I'm told—and reported the crime. The police put your name together with the theft report on the million-dollar wedding gown, and when Deputy Jim began making inquiries, he discovered you were wanted for questioning."

"On the theft?"

He nodded.

"And the kidnapping?"

"No."

But he denied it too quickly, and she realized the truth. "The police think I stole the gown and kidnapped you in the process, don't they?"

"They only want to talk to you. Leanne probably gave them your name as the woman who was with me at the church, and the misunderstanding arose from that."

Eliza scraped the toe of her saddle shoe across the floor, debating and discarding one option after another, trying to figure out how she could possibly explain her way out of this. "I'm kind of surprised that Leanne remembered my name," she said, catching the thought as it slipped by.

"Believe me, Leanne will never forget you—or forgive you." Mack ran his hand through his neatly combed hair, revealing in a gesture how worried he really was...and she loved him for caring. "But there's no way you can be blamed for the kidnapping, and I won't allow anyone to harass you about it. The stolen gown is going to be a little more difficult, but we'll figure out something. I'll offer a reward. A big one. More money than Chuck earns in an entire year."

"You can't do that."

"I can't?"

"No. You forfeited your inheritance when you married me, remember?"

A trace of a smile flitted across his mouth and disappeared. "Right. Well, luckily, I can still get my hands on enough money to make a tempting reward."

"I won't let you do that, Mack. Trying on the dress was my mistake and it is not your problem. I'll figure out something, some way to get it back." It was the only way she could prove she hadn't stolen it in the first place. "I have to get it back."

"Oh, no." Mack advanced on her like a Sherman tank and grasped her arms. "What you and I need to do next is go quietly and calmly with Sheriff Cooper. You need to be very cooperative and answer any questions he or Jim or anyone else asks you. We'll tell the truth this time—the real truth—and then the authorities can locate Chuck and get the dress back."

She looked at him, making plans fast and furiously, and doing her best to hide them from his perceptive gaze. "You honestly think they'll just ask a few questions and let me go? That's kind of optimistic, don't you think? I mean, if we try to tell the truth now, won't it just make everything worse? They might not believe either of us. And if they don't, I could be charged with grand theft and kidnapping and impersonating your wife and... and I just don't think cooperating is such a good idea."

"Eliza, for the moment, and for better or worse, I'm your husband. And no one is going to so much as look at you cross-eyed while I'm around to stop them. Understand? You and I are in this together, and no amount of explaining is going to change that."

A warmth as big as Texas swept over her. "You're one in a million, MacKenzie Cortland, and I'm honored to be your wife...even temporarily." She reached up and kissed him, fully and frankly on the mouth. Like a match to tinder, their attraction caught fire. Mack groaned softly and pulled her to him with uncompromising force. His lips on hers demanded and persuaded, sipped and plundered, denied and promised pleasures yet to be. Her impulsiveness slipped to resolve and then into sweet determination. She would

have him, no matter the cost, no matter who was hurt
or who had regrets. However transient their marriage, it was real and immediate now. And now was
the only time that mattered.

His arms tightened around her as his warm tongue
delved deeply into her mouth. A murmur of startled
pleasure tickled her throat and escaped in a sigh. His
hands dropped to her waist and slid lightly over the
contours of her hips, skimmed across the backs of her
thighs and then moved upward again in a continuous
caress. The pink dress bunched in his fingers and
slithered across her skin, a thin, sensual barrier between her and the naked delight of his touch. Breathless and aching, she grasped his hips, claiming his
passion, inviting him to claim hers. They fell back
onto the bed, onto the puffy, lumpy mattress, and
rolled with the jittery bed frame.

"Damn bed," Mack muttered, but she pressed
against him, stealing his protest with a seductive and
lengthy kiss. He responded by gathering her close,
pulling her with him into a spin of sensation and
building passion.

This was it, Eliza thought. The moment to put aside
reservations and to open herself to enjoyment, the
time to step past doubts about the future and commit
to the emotions of the present. She loved Mack for
good or ill; she loved him forever or for a day. She
belonged to him, heart and soul, even if he never truly
belonged to her in the same way. This was surrender
and victory, she thought, as she wrapped her trembling arms about his neck. This was love.

The knock on the door couldn't have been more
timely or more unwelcome. A minute longer and
Sheriff Cooper would have had to stammer out an

embarrassed apology when he opened the door and peeked in. As it was, he blushed to the roots of his sandy hair and had to clear his throat twice before he recovered his voice. "Sorry," he said, keeping his gaze on the floor. "I know this is your honeymoon and all, but if we don't get moving before Jim gets it into his wooden head that this is takin' too long, there could be heck to pay. It'd be just like my brother to rush down here with the sirens going and the lights flashing and make a mountain out of a little old molehill."

Eliza sat up, breathless and bewildered by her mix of stirred-up emotions. Mack captured her hand in his as he pushed up onto his elbows and frowned at the intruder. "I was, uh, just telling Eliza we'll have to go back to your office to answer a few questions." He lifted his shoulders in a shrug. "She needed a little... reassurance."

"Yeah." His head bent, the sheriff looked anywhere except at the bed. "I'll, uh, just be waitin' outside."

Eliza gathered her wits, slipped her hand from Mack's protective grasp and groped her way off the mattress. "We'll be out in a few minutes, Sheriff." She brushed back her tousled hair and battled the urge to look at Mack again. She had to concentrate, had to keep in touch with her quickly conceived plan and had to keep away from the distracting temptation that was Mack. "If you don't mind, I'd like to have enough time to comb my hair and freshen up a little before I have to face the inquisition."

"Sure. Sure. Take as much time as you need." Sheriff Tim backed away from the doorway. "I'll wait for you to say your goodbyes."

Goodbyes?

Mack pushed himself to his feet as the front door closed behind the sheriff. "He didn't mean that the way it sounded, Eliza. They are not going to separate us, I promise."

She smiled and took a couple of steps toward the bathroom and away from the bed. "I know. And I'm not worried. Truly. I'll just go in the bathroom, and, uh, freshen up a little...before we go. It shouldn't take more than a minute...or two. If you want to wait outside with the sheriff, I'll hurry and be out in—in a flash."

A glimmer of suspicion came and went in Mack's dark eyes, and she conjured up all the innocence she could muster. "I'll be out in a jiffy," she said. "Why don't you keep the sheriff company?"

"I'll wait here for you." Mack stood his ground, not moving a half inch toward the front door, standing solidly between her and the open window.

"You don't need to do that."

"Oh, I don't mind. And Eliza? I'll be counting the seconds."

She nodded, and her smile remained in place until she closed the bathroom door and leaned against it. She didn't know why he had to have such a suspicious nature. If he could have just gone outside for a second, she'd have been out the window and he'd have been free of her and this hopeless situation. Except...maybe it wasn't quite hopeless just yet. With a pensive gaze, she followed the line of Mack's orange coveralls—hanging across the top of the shower stall, over the sill and through the open window to the back of the cabin. Not as easy an escape as the other window, but not impossible, either. If she could get up there, she could get through that window. And she was just desperate enough to try.

When Mack opened the door and looked in, she was standing on the toilet seat, leaning across the shower stall, her hands curled over the windowsill. She didn't even glance back at him as she pushed, levered her weight with her arms and slung one leg across the sill. Tucking her skirt modestly around her thighs, she finally looked up. "Just close the door, Mack, and pretend you didn't see this. Trust me, I know what I'm doing."

"That would be a first. Now get down from there. You're not going to run off and leave me holding the bag."

She straddled the sill. "You're in the clear, Mack. No one can accuse you of stealing the dress or of anything except being in the wrong place at the wrong time. I, on the other hand, have a lot to answer for, and frankly, without that dress, I don't think there's even a remote chance I'll be believed."

"That's ridiculous. I told you I'd back you up. I'll just explain everything exactly the way it happened, and they'll have to believe me."

"Because it's the truth." God, she loved him. "Look, Mack, no offense, but when you start trying to explain the truth, everything gets very mixed up. Think about it. The reason we got married was because you insisted on telling the truth...and not even Mr. Silk believed you." She hunched her shoulders and dropped her head, prepared to clear the raised window. "Now, if you'll just let me get a decent head start..."

But he grabbed her foot before she could escape. "This is ridiculous. You can't leave. Not like this.

Sheriff Cooper and Deputy Cooper and the entire Kansas City Police Department will come after you! Don't you realize that? And how you think you can get away without being seen is beyond me. It's an insane idea, so please, just climb down from that window."

She leaned forward and put her hand over his on her shoe. "Mack, I have to get that bridal gown and see that it's put back in the right hands. Don't you see? It's the only shot I have at proving I didn't steal it in the first place."

"And how in hell do you think you can do that? Go around knocking on doors, asking for Chuck?"

"I'll think of something. Ten minutes, Mack. That's all I'm asking. And then you don't have to feel responsible for me anymore. You can go home to Leanne with a clear conscience. You can tell her I said you were a perfect gentleman and everything I ever wished for in a husband." She wrinkled her nose in wry wistfulness. "I wish with all my heart that this had been a real marriage and that you hadn't spent so much of the night sleeping."

"Eliza..."

"On second thought, you probably shouldn't tell her that last part." She blew him a kiss. "Goodbye, Mack. Thanks for sharing the best night of my whole life." Twisting her foot and flipping the pink skirt, she pulled free and slid through the opening.

The last thing he saw was the dark sole of her saddle shoe disappearing over the window ledge against a patch of jail-house orange. His hands on his hips, he stood in the bathroom, counting his frustrations, considering the unlikely prospect of her getting away from the area unseen, calculating the odds against her finding Chuck *and* the dress, contemplating the total idiocy of the whole idea, savoring the memory of that passionate kiss. He wondered if there was any way he could squeeze through that little window.

Now, why would he do something so utterly stupid? He could wait ten minutes, walk out the front door and tell Sheriff Cooper that Eliza was gone. He could get into a comfortable car and be driven home. He could pick up the reins of his life as if this little interruption had never occurred, as if Eliza had never burst in and tangled up his heart.

Reaching into the stall, he turned on the shower and shut the curtain. He pulled the bathroom door closed behind him and walked across the cabin to the window Eliza had left open. Quietly and quickly, he shut and locked it, then he picked up the phone, noted the number and, using the local prefix, dialed at random. When a man answered, he hung up and tried again.

"Hello?" This time the answering voice was soft and sweet and womanly.

He asked her to hold for Sheriff Cooper, tossed the receiver onto the bed and strode to the doorway, pausing only long enough to grab a biscuit from the tray and stuff it into his shirt pocket. "Sheriff?" Opening the door, he motioned as he stepped outside. "There's a phone call for you."

"In there?" Sheriff Tim gestured to the open doorway.

"Yes. She didn't give her name."

"She?" Tim passed him with a pleasant nod. "Okay. Thanks, I'll just go in and answer it."

"You do that." Mack nodded just as pleasantly. The moment the sheriff was inside, he closed the front door, shut the screen and wedged a stick through the metal handle. Then he raced around the corner of Cabin 5 in search of Eliza.

Chapter Twelve

Across the street at a gas pump outside the Tank 'N Tummy, a man in a blue shirt and red baseball cap finished filling the fuel tank of a battered green truck, then walked toward the store, clapping his hands and talking to someone or something out of Mack's range of vision. No sooner had the man turned away, than a dark head popped up in the window of the old truck, then bobbed out of sight again.

Who but Eliza, Mack thought, relieved to have found her so quickly. Crouched at the corner of Cabin 7, he had a good view of the gas pump, the parked truck and the big yellow sunflower painted on a window of the Sunflower Café...which just happened to be adjacent to the convenience store. A rocket scientist might never have figured it out, but he had known right off that Eliza would head back to the café on the chance she could still catch the ride to Topeka. And the lucky little "persuader" had obviously done just that, because if that wasn't her in the cab of that truck, he would eat his hat. If he had one.

Adrenaline pumping, he took just enough time to plan his route before he dashed across the street at an angle, dodged behind a car parked at the café and then raced for the truck in a scuffling, duck-and-run waddle. "Eliza?" he said quietly as he crept up beside the pickup. "Eliza!"

Keeping her head low, she peeped through the open window. "Mack! What are you doing here?"

"Ssh. I'm looking for you."

She started rolling up the window. "I am not going back with you, Mack. I'm going after the dress."

"I know. I'm coming with you."

The window stopped rising and lowered an inch. "What did you say?"

He glanced around, feeling the seconds careening past like a fire engine. "I said I'm coming with you. Scoot over."

"Get out of here. You're going to spoil my getaway."

"Eliza, let me in."

"Not by the hair of my chinny, chin, chin."

He shifted his crouched position. "I don't have enough huff-and-puff to play games, so either open this door and scoot over or get out and we'll find another way out of town."

"Oh, right, like we can just buy a ticket for the bus or hop on the nearest freight train. And I won't hitch a ride with just anyone, you know. I met Tom at breakfast. He's Arnetta's nephew, and he was nice enough to offer to take me as far as Topeka and I'm going. So go away."

"Get it through your head, I'm going with you. If he's nice enough to give you a ride, then he won't object to giving me one, too."

"Well, he might. It's pretty crowded up here when he and the dog get in."

"The dog can ride in back. Dogs love that wind-blown feeling. Now scoot over."

"Not without asking him. That would be plain rude."

"Well, it would be downright inconsiderate to leave me behind to rot in the county jail. Open that door and let me in."

"We've been over this already. You're in the clear now. Sheriff Cooper has no reason to put you in jail again, much less let you rot there."

"He didn't... until I locked him in the cabin."

"You did what?"

Glancing over his hunched shoulder, he reached for the door handle. "Where is this Tom guy, anyway? If we don't get going, we'll get caught without ever making it out of the parking lot."

"It's just like you to horn in on *my* escape. If you'd just done as I asked, if you'd given me a ten-minute head start like I wanted, no one would even know I was gone."

"Yet," he added pointedly. "And I am trying to help you... at great personal risk, I might add."

"By locking the sheriff in our cabin? I hardly think—"

"This guy botherin' you, Eliza?"

The man in the blue plaid shirt and red baseball cap approached the truck in a rambling walk just as Mack smelled a vaguely familiar odor and felt something wet smear across his forearm. Turning his head, he found himself arm to nose with the stupid yellow dog. "What are you doing here, chicken breath?"

The yellow dog barked and wagged his tail, as if he'd just met up with a long-lost litter mate.

"Well, looky there. He likes you."

Mack gazed up at the husky, muscled and thick-necked Tom and decided there was no way Eliza was going to run amok across Kansas with a man whose only references were an unknown waitress and this hayseed hound. "Is this your dog?" he asked, knowing the answer could well seal his fate.

"That's Einstein," the man said. "Aunt Arnetta's been keeping him for me, but I raised him from a pup."

"All right, Eliza." Mack straightened. "Get out of there right now. You're not going as far as the stop sign with this guy."

Eliza glowered at him. "Don't be an idiot, Mack. I am going and you're not."

Tom looked puzzled. "He wants to go to Topeka, too?"

"Yes," Eliza said. "This is Mack Cortland. Tell him he cannot come with us to Topeka."

Tom turned to Mack. "You want to go to Topeka?"

"No." He glanced back at the motel, but saw no signs of frantic activity...yet. "I don't want to go to Topeka. But I'm her husband, Tom, and where she goes, I go. So let's go."

The man shrugged. "Never let it be said that Tom Webster separated a husband and wife against their will. Hop in the back. Come on, Einstein, let's go."

Wagging his tail, the dog stopped sniffing Mack and raced around the truck, barking like an idiot. When Tom opened the driver's door, Einstein jumped into

the cab like a veteran. "I'd prefer to ride in front."
Mack leaned against the door and addressed Tom
through the open window and across Eliza. "With my
wife."

"If the two of you want to be together, then she can
get in back with you, but Einstein rides up here with
me." Tom turned on the ignition and put the trans-
mission in gear. "Either way, you better make up your
mind, 'cause we're rollin'."

Eliza looked at Mack, but made no move to get out.
The yellow dog announced his impatience with a big,
stupid, doggy grin and a series of sharp, what-are-you-
waiting-for, let's-get-going barks.

The truck lurched forward and Mack took a step
back before he decided he was down to his last option. Grabbing hold of the side, he stepped onto the
running board and vaulted into the back of the pickup.
He hunkered down at an uncomfortable angle as the
truck pulled out onto the road and sped past the cabins of the Hay Capitol Motel.

AN HOUR DOWN THE ROAD, Tom stopped to add a
quart of oil to the rattletrap engine. The yellow dog
bounded out and raced like a bullet for the nearest
wheat field. Eliza got out and stretched, while Mack
jealously eyed her seat in the cab.

"Aren't you going to get out and stretch?" she
asked pleasantly.

He wanted to, but he was afraid if he got out, his
body would never let him get back in. "I'm fine."

"You want to trade places?" She came up beside
him, propped her arms on the side of the truck, her
chin on her hands, and smiled. "I think one of us

should be in front with Tom. He talks a lot and doesn't pay enough attention to stop signs and brake lights and staying on his side of the road. But if you want to sit with him, I wouldn't mind riding back here. I think I'd like the feel of the wind in my hair."

He was sorely tempted, but he shook his head. "You're just jealous of my new windblown hairstyle."

Her eyes flirted with his. "I am. My fingers are fairly itching to tangle with it."

"That could be dangerous."

"Would be, considering the kind of tangles I make."

He could only imagine the touch of her hands in his hair...and that was most likely for the best. "You stay in the cab and keep Tom on target. I'm fine. One good thing about riding back here is the dog is up front with you."

"Good point." She glanced toward the open hood and Tom, then lowered her voice. "Just between you and me, Einstein could use a bath and a brain. And not necessarily in that order."

And just that easily, Mack recovered his good humor. He might be the first Cortland in history to be on the lam, but inexplicably, the world suddenly made sense. "Eliza? Thanks."

"Thanks?" Her laughter was warm and pleasing. "For noticing that the dog is dumb and smells bad?"

He shook his head. "For offering to trade places."

"Einstein! Let's go, Einstein!" Tom slammed the hood and whistled for the dog. "You two ready to go?" He tossed the empty can into the back, splattering oil droplets across Mack's borrowed blue jeans.

Mack factored in the cost of a new pair of jeans for Ken Cooper. "Ready," he replied.

"Ready." Eliza opened the door. "And Mack?"

His heart caught at the sight of her smile.

"You're welcome." She climbed into the cab and closed the door.

What a great day to be going to Topeka, he thought.

"Einstein!" Tom stood beside the truck, waiting for the dog he'd raised from a pup. "Let's go, buddy!"

The dog raced from the field at the same speed he'd raced in. He bounded up to the truck, promptly leapt into the back and tried to stick his nose in Mack's shirt pocket.

"Well, I'll be. He must really like you." Shaking his head, Tom got into the cab and started the engine.

By the time Mack got Einstein's muzzle out of his pocket, the biscuit was half eaten and they were on the road again with the wind in their hair.

"THANKS, TOM!" Eliza slammed the pickup door enthusiastically. "'Bye, and good luck with those cows!"

Mack climbed over the tailgate and jumped to the ground. The jolt united every muscle in his body in protest. Five hours and fifty-five minutes was too long to spend in the back of a truck bumping along at forty-plus miles an hour. Come to think of it, five minutes would have been too long. He rubbed the back of his neck and shoulders as he watched the green pickup pull out into Topeka traffic, with Einstein back inside the cab and barking a nonstop and zealous farewell.

"'Bye!" Eliza waved cheerfully. "That worked out just great, didn't it? I know hitchhiking isn't a really smart thing to do and all, but Tom was very nice. And interesting, too. He raises cows and sells them to rodeos, did you know that? No, I suppose you couldn't hear much of the conversation back there, could you?''

"Not much, no.'' Mack wasn't sure he'd ever again hear much of anything except whistling wind in his ears and Einstein's persistent barking. "The dog talked a lot, though, so I wasn't lonely.''

Eliza looked around, taking in their surroundings with a visual sweep. "Tom said he'd never seen Einstein take to anyone like he did to you.''

"Obviously not enough people carry biscuits in their pockets.''

She turned for a closer look at the strip mall behind them. "I don't think there's anyplace to get biscuits here. Are you hungry?''

As if it mattered. "You're the brains of this outfit. What do we do next?''

"I'm thinking.''

He rubbed his aching hip and watched an approaching police car. The flight-or-fight instinct kicked in and he glanced about for a place to hide...but the black-and-white vehicle cruised past without even slowing down. "Eliza, did you know that the Cortland Foundation supports a variety of law-enforcement auxiliaries and organizations?''

She stooped down and retied one shoelace. "No, I didn't know, but then, until I met you, I'd never even heard of the Cortland Foundation.''

He was surprised. "But you knew who I was right away.''

"Well, of course. I fitted you for the tux, and your name was on the ticket."

Mack liked the idea that she knew nothing about him except what she'd learned during their brief adventure. Adventure? He was standing at a four-way stop in Topeka, Kansas, wearing borrowed clothes, without a penny in his pockets, dodging police cars and waiting for Eliza to tell him what idiotic thing he was about to try next. Was this adventure or insanity?

She turned to him with a purposeful smile. "Okay, Mack, this is what we're going to do...."

INSANITY, he decided two hours later as they climbed into the cab of a huge tractor trailer parked outside a truck stop. In his entire life, he'd never even been close to a rig this size, and now he was hitching a ride with a woman driver who didn't look big enough to handle a go-cart.

"I'm Ruth," she said. "I can take you as far as Lawrence."

"Great." Eliza couldn't have looked more delighted. "I'm Eliza. He's Mack. I had no idea these trucks would be so cozy inside."

"Take a look in the back," Ruth suggested, indicating a curtained area behind the seats.

Eliza didn't wait for a second invitation. "You have everything in here."

"Except the kitchen sink...which is fine with me. I never liked to cook, anyway." Ruth laughed, and the big engine purred. "This truck has all the comforts of home. Handsome and I travel in style."

"Handsome?" Mack asked.

A cocker spaniel poked his head through the curtain, sniffed the air and promptly nuzzled his way over Mack's shoulder and down to his pocket.

"You must have a way with animals." Ruth nodded her approval and drove out of the parking lot.

"I'M BEGINNING TO THINK I was totally wrong about hitchhiking." Eliza watched the twin exhaust pipes of the Babe Ruth Express as the semi rolled on down the highway, leaving them at an intersection anchored by a pizzeria, a submarine-sandwich shop, a Taco Casa and a coin-operated laundry. "In just two experiences I've met Tom and Ruth, two very nice and interesting people. And I've learned all about raising rodeo cows and how to drive a big rig."

"Bulls." Mack looked around for a taxi. At this point—a mile or so inside the city limits of Lawrence—he figured they were close enough to Kansas City to hire a cab and pay the fare once they reached home.

"I beg your pardon," Eliza said with an offended sniff. "Just because I didn't actually *drive* the truck doesn't mean I didn't learn something about *how* to drive it. If I had to, you know. I mean, in an emergency or something, I think I could—"

"I didn't say bull, as in 'I doubt it.' I said bulls, as in he raises bulls, not cows."

"Oh." She frowned. "Well, you can't have bulls without cows, so Tom must raise them, too."

"Knowing how fond you are of cows, I'm surprised you didn't make a date to visit his ranch."

"I don't have to see the ranch to be interested in it." She looked across the street. "I bet they have good pizza there."

He followed her gaze to the pizzeria, and his stomach gave a long, low grumble. "Don't think about food. Think about how we're going to get home from here."

She sighed. "Find a semi and I'll drive us right out of here."

"Too bad we don't have a CB radio so you could just call up one of your new buddies. You were quite a hit on the trucker channel. How many marriage proposals did you get?"

Her lips tightened. "You know as well as I do that they were just joking around. I'll bet every one of those guys is married."

"I'll bet you are, too."

Her eyes widened. "I forgot. I am married. I guess I just don't *feel* married."

A car sped past, whipping up a dust devil around his ankles. "How does being married feel?"

Shifting her weight from one saddle oxford to the other, she leaned out and looked down the street, presumably searching for another semi. "Now how would I know?"

He wanted to kiss her right there, right then, and make her so weak with desire she'd know what it meant to be married to him, whether she felt that way or not. But it was a street corner and he was a Cortland. "Just think, if you hadn't already married me, you could be watching the sunset from the cab of an eighteen-wheeler, snuggled next to Mighty Moose or Alabama Jimmy."

"It was Mighty Mike," she said in a snippy voice. "And if he'd had a pizza, I'd have gone with him anywhere."

"Yes, well, so would I." Mack manfully ignored the smells wafting his way and looked for a sign indicating a public telephone. "I'm going to call a cab."

"But we don't have any money."

"We'll pay when we get home."

"Can we do that?" She frowned as she lifted the hem of her skirt and absently scratched her thigh. "Won't they ask for a deposit or credit or some kind of collateral?"

"We'll tell the truth and—"

Her skeptical look silenced him, and into the momentary lull, four cars zoomed to a standstill in front of them. "Hey!" someone yelled. "Going our way?"

"So, DOES THIS Carter Foundation give very good scholarships? Because if it's less than a thousand, I just don't think it's worth filling out all that paperwork and stuff, you know? I mean, if it takes up too much of my time and all, then it's like it's just not cost effective, you know?"

Between Dave, a psychology major at KU, and Dan, whose career field was as yet undecided, Mack was scrunched in the front seat of a modestly souped-up Dodge. In the back seat were, respectively, Wes, Sean and Brian. They were all brothers in the same fraternity and on their way to Kansas City to participate in a male-bonding experience known as summer rush. Up ahead, darting in and out of traffic like a firefly, was a brilliant green Camaro, the leader of the fraternal caravan and the vehicle in which Eliza had chosen to ride. Mack could only hope she was wearing a seat belt.

"So, you know, like what kind of application do you have to fill out? For that Carter Foundation place you work at?" Brian, whose major had mercifully slipped Mack's mind, persisted. "And how long does it take to get the money?"

"It's the Cortland Foundation and it doesn't grant scholarships." He wiggled his shoulders and tried not to notice that the Camaro was pulling some distance ahead of the other cars in the caravan. "There'd be no point in your filling out an application."

"You mean you don't help people go to college and better themselves and get ahead in the world?"

Mack had never been more thankful for the foundation's guidelines. "That's right. Sorry."

"Well, so, maybe you ought to change that. I mean, college students have a tough time paying for their education, you know."

The Camaro slowed down and the Dodge moved closer again. "What's Boomer doing up there?" Dan, the driver of the Dodge, said to no one in particular. "He's practically backing up."

Dave, the psych major, leaned across Mack to speak to Dan. "I think he wants to talk to us. Roll down your window."

"Is that a good idea?" Mack tried to suggest that conversation between two moving vehicles was not an effective or safe means of communication. "Why don't we just pull over?"

Dan, impervious to subtlety, rolled down the window as the Dodge pulled up beside the Camaro.

"Mack!" Eliza cupped her hands around her mouth and leaned across a husky, good-looking young man. "Boomer invited me to the hot-wheels party!" She pointed at the laughing young man behind the steering wheel. "Everyone has to wear a car accessory! Isn't that cute?"

He couldn't believe she was yelling at him from the next lane of traffic.

Sean leaned forward. "What are you gonna wear, Eliza?" he hollered, nearly deafening Mack in one ear. "I'll be the one with the antenna!"

She laughed, said something to the young men in the Camaro, and they laughed, too. "Mack!" She cupped her hands around her happy grin. "We can go as matching seat covers!"

Dan shook his head and sped up to keep even with the Camaro. "He's not invited!"

"Yeah," Brian yelled from the back seat. "He's not invited!" He poked Mack on the shoulder. "You really ought to change your mind and give out a few scholarships. Then you might get into some really cool parties."

"Mack!" Eliza yelled again. "Look! Chee-tos!" She held up a crumpled bag of snacks. "Catch!"

Before he guessed her intention, she threw the bag through the window. Dan stretched out his hand to catch it, but they escaped in a flurry of bright orange curls and scattered down the highway.

"Sorry...!" Eliza called as the Camaro zoomed on ahead in a streak of brilliant green.

Mack eyed the lone Chee-to that had blown onto the dashboard, but before he could grab it, Dan picked it up and ate it.

"I saw how they make Chee-tos once," Wes said from the back. "It was way cool how they finally come out on this little track thing, all puffed up and cheesy and hot. I ever tell you guys I saw that?"

"Only a million times."

"You told us."

"I hope she comes to the party."

Dave looked longingly after the Camaro's green blur. "I wish she was riding with us."

It was the first statement in over an hour with which Mack wholeheartedly agreed.

"THIS HAS BEEN a great day." Eliza pushed the recliner into the full-stretch position and put her hands behind her head. "But I have never been so glad to be home."

Home was a small, squat, but charming older house in Kansas City, to which they'd been delivered some time ago by the testosterone-driven Camaro and the nerdy brown Dodge. Mack finished his sandwich and settled back with his cup of coffee. With the edge off his hunger and a comfortable chair to sit in, he relaxed enough to appreciate the place Eliza called home. It looked like her, he thought. All mismatched colors and a collage of styles that somehow blended into an aesthetic whole. Nothing fit, but nothing seemed out of place, either. "I like what you've done with the house," he said.

"Thanks, I like the way it's developing, myself. My friends thought I was crazy to move out of my apartment and into this place. It's one of those lease-purchase deals, and I can fix up the place in exchange for paying lower rent. My home-improvement budget is pretty skimpy, since I'm trying to save money to open my own bridal shop, but I manage to do a little something every month. Anyway, the price was right and Auntie Gem thought it was a good idea. She's always telling me it will be hard to follow my heart if I can't balance my checkbook."

"Very profound. I'd like to meet your Auntie Gem."

"I have a feeling the two of you would like each other. I have to warn you, though, she doesn't make any better sense in person."

"I like her already." He propped his feet on the hassock. "And she made perfect sense if she guided you to buy this house. It suits you."

"Maybe. I prefer to believe I suit the house. I think sometimes people spend so much time trying to find what suits them, they miss out on the chance to discover they actually suit what has found them."

"Another Auntie Gem-ism? Or is that strictly Eliza?"

"A little of both, I'm afraid. Occasionally, even I'm not sure what I'm saying." She yawned and stretched before folding her hands in her lap. "Feel free to make more coffee if you want," she offered, snuggling deeper into the recliner. "Or another sandwich."

"I'll just sit here, thanks. It's been a long day."

"A great day." Her voice was soft and sleepy.

He noticed the droop of her eyelids, the slow, steady rise and fall of her breasts. The moment they'd hit the door, she'd directed him to the kitchen, while she headed for the bathroom and a shower. Now her hair was wet and clingy, her face scrubbed as clean as a daisy, her body damp and tempting beneath a loose

T-shirt and jumper. A sigh slipped past her lips and her head lolled to the side.

Feeling comfortable and contented, Mack sipped his coffee and watched her sleep...and knew for the first time in his life that he suited what had found him.

"ELIZA?" Mack stooped beside the recliner and stroked the soft inner skin of her arm. "Eliza, wake up. You're going to have an awful crick in your neck if you don't get out of this chair."

The recliner snapped upright and she sat up abruptly, startled and wide-eyed. "What? Is he here?"

"Who?"

Turning her head, she looked at him and blinked. "Mack?"

He smiled. "At least you didn't scream this time."

"I don't scream . . . do I?"

"Yes, you do, and I have the scars to prove it."

"Did you make me scream?"

"Not yet, but I'm thinking about it."

His meaning seemed to slip into the fog of her sleepy brain and get lost there, because her gaze moved from him to the familiar furnishings. "Oh, we're home. Is it morning already? I've got to get up and call the limousine service. We have to find out if Chuck brought the limo back here or drove it to California or did something else with—"

"It's barely past ten." He reached up and smoothed the furrows from her brow. "You fell asleep in the chair, and I thought you'd be more comfortable in bed, that's all."

She pushed a distracted hand through her hair. "It's not time to go after the dress?"

He shook his head. "It's time to go to bed."

"Bed," she repeated with a yawn. "Oh, you should have just wandered into one of the bedrooms and gone on to bed. I can sleep anywhere. Sometimes I go days at a time without getting into a bed."

"Well, tonight isn't one of those days. It hurts my neck just to watch you." He pushed himself to his feet, reached for her hand and tugged. "Come on."

Eliza resisted, feeling rested and anxious and confused all at the same time. "Wait a minute. You woke me up to tell me to go to bed?"

"You've been asleep in that chair for over an hour."

"This isn't going to turn into another I-slept-more-than-you-slept argument, is it?"

"If you'll recall, that argument had very little to do with sleep."

A sudden, prickly awareness assailed her. "Oh. Right. It was about cold showers, wasn't it?"

"Not exactly." He gave her hand another, more-forceful tug. "And I'm not sure you want this discussion to go any further."

"Oh, I don't know. I have lots of cold water."

He regarded her for a moment, then cupped her chin in the palm of his hand and gently compelled her to stand. "That's good, because you may very well need it."

Her heart barely stammered out a two-step beat of anticipation and protest before he claimed her in a long, wet, thorough kiss. Then, before she could catch her breath, he did it again. Her lips couldn't help but respond to his persuasion as a sweet weakness permeated her body and she was forced to put her arms around him for balance. His form pressed hard and purposefully against hers, providing a devastating blow to her resolve. Mack wanted her. She wanted him. Wasn't that all that mattered?

"Mack." She slipped her hands between them and pressed on his chest. "I can't sleep with you. You don't belong to me."

"I do tonight." He lifted her in his arms. "Which door leads to the bedroom?"

"That one." She pointed and told herself she had every right to spend the night with him. One night out of all the rest of the nights in his life. One night to claim him as her husband, as her lover. But when he laid her down on the bed and stopped to take off his boots, she knew she had to be honest with herself...even if she would regret it every minute of every night for the rest of her life.

"Mack?" She touched his arm, and one boot dropped to the floor. "I don't want this."

"What? This?" He bent and kissed her with lingering hunger. "Or this?" His hand cupped her breast; his thumb stroked lightly across her nipple. "Or this?" His tongue traveled a tender distance to tease her earlobe and send shivers of longing coursing through her. "Or this?" Dropping the other boot, he stretched out beside her on the bed, gathered her into his arms and seared her with a devastating caress that burned reason into ambiguity and principle into relentless passion.

Her fingers in his hair, she kissed him and held him close and told her heart it didn't matter if this experience wouldn't be the lovemaking she'd imagined. It would mean no less to her because it was merely sex for him. Love wasn't an equal-opportunity experience. He didn't have to love her in order for the act to have meaning. She loved him enough to make it right, to forget that he really belonged to Leanne.

His lips returned to hers, gentle and insistent. She breathed in his scent, savored the touch of his hands on her body and then regretfully, resolutely pulled away. "I can't do this. I want to, but I can't."

He looked into her eyes. Pushing up, he sat beside her, but kept his hands pressed into the mattress on either side of her shoulders. "I'm sorry. I should have realized we didn't have protection, that you wouldn't be prepared."

"Protection?" she repeated. "We need *protection?* I don't have a gun or pistol or anything, but there's a broom on the back porch."

His smile was quick, but tender. "I was referring to a, uh, different kind of protection," he said gently. "More like preventing pregnancy rather than discouraging prowlers."

Of course. She felt the heat of embarrassment as it spread under her skin in a soft, warm rush. "Oh," she muttered. "Oh. *That* kind of prepared. I see. I thought you meant... Well, I was thinking about Leanne, you see, and wondering what she'd do if she found out that we—that you... And I thought she might... well, come over here and be mad and... I guess she wouldn't do that... would she?"

He touched her hair, looping a wayward strand behind her ear with a light and incredibly seductive movement. She could barely breathe for looking at him, and at that moment she would have willingly forsworn chocolate for the rest of her life if only she could taste his kiss. "No," he said quietly. "It wouldn't be in character for her to follow a man and wife into their bedroom."

Eliza swallowed hard. "But . . . she's your fiancée."

"I believe having a wife pretty much wipes out any previous engagement."

"But, Mack, you made a commitment to her you never made to me. We can't just pretend that it was cancelled out by a marriage that is nothing but a pretense."

He leaned closer, his gaze holding hers, his chest only inches away from the rapid rise and fall of her breasts. "It doesn't feel like a pretense." His lips grazed hers with temptation. "In fact, I'm beginning to feel very married."

She swallowed and managed to produce a quivery whisper. "How does it feel to be . . . married?"

He stroked her cheek with his thumb. "I can explain it, if you'd like. Just say the word."

Could she? Should she? "Protection?" she asked.

His sigh warmed her lips and he slowly drew back to look down at her. "That wasn't the word I had in mind, but it's pretty persuasive. Are you saying you don't have any kind of protection?"

Sincere regret flooded through her. "The broom is about the only protective device in the whole house. Unless you count the mousetrap under the kitchen sink."

"I wouldn't want to count that, no." He rolled over and dropped beside her onto the mattress. "I could go to a drugstore."

"No, you can't. It's too far to walk, and my car's still at the boutique." She touched his arm lightly, hesitantly offering to share his frustration. "Maybe it's for the best, Mack. I mean, sex always complicates relationships. It says so in all the women's magazines. And besides, just because we've been through a lot together and we're feeling sort of *attached,* who's to say we'll feel that way tomorrow? I mean, after we've located the dress and everything's been explained and everyone understands, you might be thanking your lucky stars that you're not involved with me for another second."

"Maybe you'll be the thankful one."

"I already am," she said softly. He drew back, a frown beginning in his eyes and on his mouth, but she lifted her hand to touch his cheek and to keep him from moving farther away. "I'm thankful to have accidentally fallen into your life. Thankful that we shared a handful of hours. Thankful that the Worth gown brought me a lot of trouble and at least a million dollars worth of memories."

He turned his head to press a kiss into her palm, and a dewy pleasure unfolded like morning inside her. "Eliza," he whispered. "My million-dollar bride."

The words, the tenderness in his voice, the desire in his eyes combined to produce the most seductive, sensual yearning she'd ever known. She sighed with excruciating regret. "You'd think for that much money you'd get better protection than a broom."

"Maybe you should hit me with a frying pan and put me out of my misery for the night."

She winced at the thought. "The other bedroom is through that door and down the hall to the left. You should probably go there before I start imagining new ways to make you miserable."

He didn't even give the open doorway a glance. "I'm not going to another bedroom. I'm staying here...with my wife." Rolling onto his side, he cupped her chin in his hand. "If I'm going to be miserable, you can bet that you are, too."

"Mack, we can't spend another night watching each other not sleep and taking turns in the shower. That will only make us tired and cranky and run up the water bill."

His smile was full of slow amusement and devastating intentions. "Then we'll just have to think of something else to do. Something involving your lips..." He leaned closer. "...and my lips..." Her heart nearly burst with anticipation. "...and your body..." His warm breath mingled with hers. "...and my lips..."

She managed to slip her fingertip between his lips and hers. "But we can't. We don't have any—"

"...and your fingers...and my lips...." He took her fingertip into his mouth and sucked lightly...and she forgot how to talk. A dizzy moment later, he kissed an erotic path from her lips to the hollow below her ear. "There are other ways to feel married, Eliza," he whispered. "Let me explain...."

And to her astonished delight, he proved he was very good with explanations.

Chapter Thirteen

"Are you sure they said 'Chuck'?"

Eliza stopped looking out the front window long enough to frown at Mack. "For the hundredth time, yes. That isn't a name I'm likely to misunderstand."

"I just can't believe he got up this morning and decided to go to work."

"He didn't. I explained to the manager of the limousine service that I was a friend of his and that I was only going to be in Kansas City this one day and I'd really appreciate it if he could put me in touch with him. Then the manager asked me if I needed a limo while I was in town, and I said, only if I can hire Chuck to drive me around. Then I laughed, kind of like this...." She demonstrated. "And I said it would be worth a hundred dollars to me just to see the look on Chuck's face when he found out I had hired him." She turned back to the window. "I was really tempted to say it would be worth a million bucks, but I was afraid the manager wouldn't take me seriously."

"He bit for the extra hundred?"

"He nibbled. That's when I said—very softly, like I was just talking to myself—that I'd give ten times that amount just to be able to surprise Chuck and spend a couple of hours alone with him. The service manager couldn't get my credit-card number printed onto that invoice fast enough, and he promised Chuck would be here in an hour if he had to send him special delivery.''

"You're paying a thousand dollars on the slight chance that this guy will actually be able to find Chuck and send him over here?''

"No, we settled on two hundred fifty, plus the normal rental charge.''

"I think that's illegal.''

"He quoted a price and I agreed to it. There's nothing illegal about that.''

"It's unethical, and I can't believe you'd stoop to bribery.''

"I may spend the next thirty years in prison for trying on a wedding dress and getting mixed up in a kidnapping. Bribery is small potatoes on my road to ruin, believe me.''

"You're not going to prison, but you probably are going to lose your two hundred fifty dollars.''

"Actually, I was planning to borrow that much from you. But I'll pay you back...no matter how long it takes. Don't worry, though, I have a good feeling about this.''

"I don't know how you can be optimistic." Mack came to stand behind her and look over her shoulder out the window. A delicious quiver shimmied through her with his nearness, and she leaned ever so slightly against his broad, warm chest, acknowledging her memories of last night and the hope that, later, after they recovered the dress and resolved their immediate problems, he would still want her.

"Even if Chuck is in town," Mack continued, "I can't imagine he's dumb enough to pick up a fare, especially one that requested him by name. He must know we'd be looking for him."

"It makes more sense to me that he'd want everything to appear normal."

"I don't think he's that smart."

She glanced up. "Why don't you have another cup of coffee while we're waiting?"

"No, thanks, I've had my quota this morning. So you honestly think he'll just drive up to your house?"

"Yes, I do. It's only a hunch, but yes, I think there's a better-than-even chance he will be here within the next ten minutes."

"And what's the plan if he doesn't?"

"Why don't you check your pocket? Surely there's a plan in there somewhere."

"Very funny. Maybe I will have another cup of coffee."

A limousine turned the corner and drove slowly down the street toward the house. Eliza smiled and let the curtain drop into place. "Forget the coffee," she said. "It's showtime."

CHUCK TOOK ONE LOOK at her and went pale. "I must have the wrong address."

"Oh, no," she said, smiling as she moved down the walk toward him. "You're at the right place and you're right on time, too."

He turned on his heel, but Mack had gone out the back of the house, circled the limousine and now was leaning against the driver's door. "Hello, Chuck," he said. "Going my way?"

"Now, look..." Chuck glanced from her to Mack. "You probably aren't going to believe this, but I was just thinkin' I owed you two a big apology."

"Really?" Mack smiled. "Let's hear it."

"Yes, I can't wait to hear it," Eliza agreed, coming up behind Chuck and poking him with the handle of her hairbrush. "Get in the car."

He jumped and stumbled toward the limo. "You've got this all wrong."

"And we're going to give you every opportunity to convince us how, Chuck." Mack opened the rear door. "Get in. We're going for a little drive."

"I'm not goin' anywhere with you."

"Get in." Eliza gave him another poke with the hairbrush. "It's our turn to chauffeur you around town."

"But—but...I'm the only one who can drive this limo. That's company policy."

"Is it, now?" Mack gestured toward the back seat. "Well, you know, Chuck, I've been thinking I need to find out what the official company policy is on kidnapping customers."

"That was just a joke. I didn't hurt you or anything. And you're home again." He laughed nervously. "No harm done. Just a joke, see?"

Mack clamped his hand on Chuck's shoulder. "I'm not sure who enjoyed the punchline more, me or Eliza. Now, get in the limo before I decide to turn your sorry butt over to the FBI." Chuck's hand clenched, but Mack was quick and sidestepped out of swinging range. "Now, now, Chuck, didn't anyone ever tell you

that you should never take a swing at the person
you're trying to apologize to? Eliza and I just want to
have a little chat with you. Nothing to be upset about.
We have a little . . . proposition for you."

"Proposition?" He looked skeptically from him to
Eliza. "What kind of proposition?"

"An exchange kind of proposition," she said,
moving to the front passenger door. "You give us
something we want and we give you something you
want."

"You haven't got anything I want."

"Ah, now, let's not be too quick." Mack kept the
chauffeur cornered between the rear door and the
limousine body. "Hear us out before you start talking like James Cagney."

Chuck's mouth pursed with rebellious indecision.
"You're wantin' me to hand over the million-dollar
dress. That's it, isn't it?"

"Get in the car," Mack said in a no-nonsense voice.

"But you want the dress back?" His question
seemed curiously intense. "You're not going to let me
keep it, are you?"

"You know you have to return the dress, Chuck.
That's a given."

Chuck sighed, nodded and almost smiled. "Okay,
then. Let's go." He got into the vehicle and, with a
puzzled look, Mack closed the door. He looked across
the sleek gray roof at Eliza and shrugged. "The pi-
geon has landed, but stay alert. He can't be trusted."

She opened the car door and slid into the front seat,
her hand briefly brushing Mack's as he got in behind
the wheel. He pressed the automatic lock, turned the
key and put the limousine in gear.

"Okay," Chuck said. "You got me out here. What's the deal?"

"All in good time." She assumed an authoritative tone as she shifted in the seat so she could keep an eye on Chuck. "Where's the dress?"

Chuck turned and stared out the window. When he looked at her again, there was something akin to relief in his eyes. "It's in the trunk."

She and Mack exchanged a quick, incredulous look. "This trunk?" Mack asked suspiciously. "You expect us to believe you're carrying it around in the trunk of this limousine?"

"I was going to find someplace to dump it."

"Right," Mack drawled. "After all the trouble you went to to get it."

"I know. And if I was you, I probably wouldn't trust me, either. But you've got to believe me. My life has been hell since I got my hands on that crummy dress."

Eliza exchanged a quick, confused look with Mack.

"Yeah," Chuck continued. "In the last twenty-four hours, the screwiest things have been happening to me. It's like I'm in the *Twilight Zone* or something."

Mack checked the rearview mirror. "What are you, a kidnapper with a guilty conscience?"

"No." Chuck shook his head. "No, it's worse than that. It's my ex-wife."

"Your ex-wife has the dress?" Mack asked.

"The dress is in the trunk. I already told you that. I snuck it out of the apartment this morning when Shelly was in the shower."

"Shelly is your ex-wife?"

"No. Shelly is my girlfriend. *Ex*-girlfriend, that is. You see, Shelly thought I bought the dress for her, and when she seen it, she starts dancing around and asking me when we're gonna get married and how many bridesmaids she ought to have, and I'm trying to tell her the dress isn't for her. But she won't believe me, thinks I'm teasing, and then nothing will do but she has to put the dress on. And just as she gets all the buttons done up, Cynthia shows up."

"Cynthia?" Eliza asked.

"Cynthia," he confirmed sadly. "My ex-wife. Well, she takes one look at Shelly in the million-dollar dress and busts right out into tears, sayin' really dumb stuff like how she had come back because she wanted our marriage to work and how she thinks we ought to try counseling." He looked at Eliza. "You coulda knocked me over with an ostrich feather. We've been divorced four years and she's not had a good word to say about me in five. And suddenly she's in my apartment and crying because she thinks I'm getting ready to marry Shelly. All this time I'm talking to Cynthia, Shelly is admiring herself in the mirror. At least I think that's what she's doing, but then all of a sudden, she busts out crying and tells me she can't marry me because she's got to marry my best friend, and she's sorry that I bought the wedding dress for her. So I say, I didn't buy the dress for her, and Cynthia somehow thinks that means I bought it for *her*. Then the next thing I know *she's* trying on the dress and looking in the mirror and crying some more and saying she and I was meant to be together and our marriage is worth saving. And I'm listening to all this and thinkin' I'm in some weird sort of parallel universe or something, and I figure the only way I'm going to get out is to get rid of the million-dollar dress.''

Eliza put her chin in her hands and stared at Chuck over the seat back. "So, you think all of this happened because of the dress?''

"Hey, I never had this kind of trouble before I laid eyes on that weddin' gown.''

Mack shrugged. "I can relate to that.''

Eliza turned her gaze on him. "What do you mean by that?''

"Nothing.'' His cocky smile charmed her all the way to her too easily impressed toes. "Nothing at all, Mrs. Cortland.''

"Mrs. Cortland?'' Chuck repeated from the back seat.

"Don't ask,'' Mack warned. "It'll only reinforce your parallel-universe theory.''

Chuck shook his head. "I'm tellin' you there's something very weird about that dress. And I'll do anything you want if you'll just take it and get it out of my life before I do something really stupid.''

"Like going to counseling with your ex-wife?'' Eliza suggested.

His sigh held a noticeable trace of resignation. "Something really stupid. Like marrying her again.''

"YOU'RE RETURNING the dress?'' Mrs. Pageatt looked from Chuck to Mack to Eliza. "All three of you?''

Eliza began the explanation. "Well, I tried it on and got the sleeve caught.''

"Then I tried to help her and got tangled up in it,'' Mack continued.

"And then I got the dumb idea of hijacking them to get the dress." Chuck shoved his hands into his pockets. "I thought I could make some easy money, turn it in for a reward or something, but then Cynthia showed up again and I think I'd be better off just goin' to jail for a few years."

Mrs. Pageatt frowned in confusion, started to say something, then opened the cardboard box and lifted out the gown. "Was the dress damaged during all this . . . tangling up?"

"No, ma'am," Chuck stated flatly. "I checked it over very carefully before I stuffed it in that box. I didn't want anybody accusing me later of tearing it or anything."

She held the gown against her and gave it a thorough going over. "Amazing, but it looks as good as new. Wrinkled, but basically fine."

"Well, that's another thing," Chuck said. "The dress keeps changing. It fit Shelly, my ex-girlfriend, like it was made for her. And then when Cynthia, my ex-wife, tried on the dress, it fit her, too. And they ain't even close to being the same size."

"It fit me, too." Eliza touched the dress lightly, wishing with all her heart she could see herself in it just once more. "I thought it was the most beautiful dress I've ever worn."

"You looked breathtaking." Mack's comment was soft with memory.

"You know, it's funny." Chuck took his hands out of his pockets and touched one lace sleeve. "Now that I think about it, Cynthia looked real pretty in that dress. Kind of made me want to . . . well, anyway, it wasn't that flattering on Shelly."

With a secret smile, Mrs. Pageatt held the dress against her own rounded shoulders. "Eliza, I think you should go in the back and put the gown on...just so we can be sure there's been no damage done, nothing we've overlooked. Do you mind?"

"No, of course not." She was more than a little puzzled by Mrs. Pageatt's odd suggestion and totally surprised by her calm acceptance of their explanation. And, if she wasn't mistaken, Eliza thought there was a definite aura of calm happiness surrounding Mrs. P. this morning. "But are you sure you want me to put it on? I could just go over the material very carefully and—"

The boutique owner thrust the gown into Eliza's hands, and her normal tone of command returned. "Put it on and come out here to the triple mirrors so we can all see you. Gentlemen, if you'd sit over there?" She gestured toward a couple of chairs. "I have to make a phone call."

Nervously, Eliza gathered the Worth gown into her arms. "A phone call?" she asked. "Are you calling the...police?"

"Yes," Mrs. Pageatt said brightly. "Well, actually, just one. The policeman who investigated the supposed theft Saturday. I want you to meet him."

Eliza gulped.

"Wait a minute," Mack said. "I believe we can explain everything to your satisfaction without involving the law."

Mrs. Pageatt gave him a soft, dreamy smile. "I'm sure you can, but Joe needs to hear this explanation, too. You see, he's someone I knew before. A long time ago. And when he walked in those doors, it was like a—a..."

"Parallel universe?" Chuck suggested.

"A miracle," she finished. "I hadn't seen him since high school, but I'd never forgotten him, even when I was married to Mr. Pageatt. And when the Worth gown came in, I couldn't resist trying it on, and then I looked in the mirror and—"

"And there he was," Eliza whispered, sharing her own experience with the older woman in a brief, but telling look.

"Yes." Mrs. Pageatt nodded slowly as a sweet smile toyed with her rouged lips. "You can't know how strange it was to see him walk through that door in person. I thought I was hallucinating again, but he was just as thunderstruck to see me as I was him, and the long and short of it is that we realized life is too brief to spend questioning whatever fates brought us back together and—" her smile broke forth like a sunbeam "—well, we're going to be married this coming Saturday."

Eliza clutched the magic wedding gown against her as she moved to hug her boss. "That's wonderful," she said. "I'm so happy for you."

Mrs. P. nodded. "Now, go on. Try on that dress. Let's see how it fits you."

With a happy smile, Eliza picked up the rumpled veil and headed for the dressing room. Maybe Chuck was right. Maybe this was a parallel universe, where everything could be put right with a few words of explanation, where the love stitched into a wedding gown could change the destinies of those who came into contact with it. Or maybe the wedding gown just had the ability to incite her imagination...and Mack's...and Mrs. Pageatt's and Chuck's. No, there was definitely something wonderfully mysterious about the million-dollar dress. And she was going to wear it one more time....

"MRS. PAGEATT ASKED ME to come back and see if you needed any..." Mack's voice trailed into a heart-stopping silence as he caught sight of Eliza.

She turned toward him, a vision in old lace and satin, and he thought he would never catch his breath again.

"Could you finish doing up the back?" she asked, as if she hadn't noticed his stunned admiration. "I think I missed a couple of buttons."

Unable to take his eyes off her, he stepped up behind her on the platform and silently fastened the remaining buttons. His hands trembled and he slowly lifted his eyes to meet hers in the mirror. Love looked back at him from her reflection, welcoming, warm and wonderful.

"Tell me what you see," she said. "In the mirror."

The woman he saw was beautiful beyond the scope of any words that came to mind. And he never wanted to be separated from her, no matter what she was—or wasn't—wearing. "I see the love of my life. I see you, Eliza. I see...my wife."

"And what would you see if I took off the dress?"

"The same thing, only naked." He smiled wickedly, tenderly. "As a matter of fact, why don't you take it off? I have this unhealthy fear of getting tangled up in it again before I can get you out of it."

She frowned at him in the mirror. "You're already in the biggest tangle of your life and you don't seem to be struggling to get free."

"As if I could ever be free of you, Eliza," he said, brooking no argument. "I love you. Will you be my wife...now and forever?"

"Mack, I—I love you, too. But what about Leanne?"

"She has no relevance in this discussion. I was having doubts about the marriage even before I met you, but I'd convinced myself that it was prewedding jitters. I wasn't in love with her then and I'm not now." He bent his head and nibbled on her ear. "How could I be when we make such a perfect couple?"

"Perfect? You think we're perfect?"

"Eliza," he said with mild reproof. "Never, ever, argue with a reflection."

She sighed with pleasure. "We do look rather beautiful, don't we?"

"Breathtaking," he said, and turned her in his arms. "You are the best thing that has ever happened to me. I had no idea love could be such an adventure or that it would hit me over the head like a frying pan." His fingertip traced the quivering softness of her lips. "In two days, you persuaded me to feel emotions I'd long given up on ever experiencing, and you won a commitment from my heart that overshadows every other obligation in my life. Then, out of the blue, you dived headfirst into my limousine and tangled me up in your lace and your laughter and made me realize how—"

"Shut up, Mack," she said.

And then she kissed him.

Chapter Fourteen

"I can't stop thinking about that clerk at the Starz Laundry." Eliza put her hand on Mack's arm before he got out of the car. "Are you sure she wrote down the right name on the ticket? She acted so goofy."

"My suave charm has that affect on women." Mack leaned over and kissed her lightly on the nose. "See? Now you're cross-eyed."

"But we promised Mrs. Pageatt we'd deliver the dress to the dry cleaners and make sure they understood when it would be picked up and who would pick it up and what they were supposed to do with it. I'm not sure that clerk even understands what day it is."

Mack laughed in the soft darkness inside the car. "You're beginning to sound like a Cortland already. I just wish you'd developed this family trait of responsible worrying when we were still in Kansas City, instead of several hours into our honeymoon. We're a long way from home and we are not driving all the way back just to check on the status of a dress we left to be dry-cleaned."

"I know...and I don't know why I keep thinking about it. Except that the clerk didn't act like she was paying the least bit of attention, and I just have this funny feeling . . .''

"Eliza, the dress is at the dry cleaners where it will be safely cleaned and stored until the new owner sends someone from California to pick it up. You and I both heard Mrs. Pageatt making the arrangements over the phone before we left the shop. Besides, no one except us and the owners know how valuable the Worth gown actually is. Chuck knows, but he wouldn't go near that dress again for a million dollars.''

She laughed with Mack. "It's too late for him, anyway. I bet he'll be married to his ex-wife before we get back from our honeymoon.''

"I certainly hope so." Mack ran his hand over her disheveled hair, his eyes full of love. "Because we're not going back for a very long time.''

"And there's no reason even to think about the million-dollar dress.''

"None at all. We did our part. We dropped off the dress, and no matter what happens to it at this point, it doesn't affect us or our honeymoon or the rest of our lives.''

"You're right," she said, brightening. "I'm being as silly as that clerk. I mean, it's not like we need the gown or anything. We're already married.''

"And thank God for that." He stroked his thumb across her cheek, and her whole body became suffused with a soft, desperate desire. "If Miz Vangie and the Cooper boys were here, I'd thank them, too.''

"Don't leave out Mr. Silk and Einstein, Tom and Ruth and the rowdy boys of Sigma Kappa, and Chuck, Mrs. Pageatt and Joe." Her smile curved in the dark. "The circle gets wider and wider. Do you think maybe Chuck was right and that everybody who comes into contact with the million-dollar dress falls in love?"

Mack curled a lock of her hair around his finger. "I think I prefer the parallel-universe theory."

She wrinkled her nose at him. "I hope Leanne meant what she said to you. I'd hate to think that anyone could be unhappy tonight."

"She'll be married to Martin York within three months," Mack predicted confidently. "When I left her this afternoon, Martin was just arriving, and he looked like he wanted to punch me in the nose. But I told him I was married—happily married—to you, and that Leanne needed a friend. That's when he shook my hand and wished us every happiness. If I'd been a little more observant earlier on, I might have figured out that he was in love with her before I asked him to be the best man at our wedding."

"Another happy ending," Eliza said with a dreamy sigh. "Maybe we'll recommend the Hay Capitol Motel to them as a great place to spend their honeymoon."

"Martin's a pilot for TWA. Leanne may have to overcome her fear of flying."

"I have a fear of not making it to a bed tonight. Why don't you go into the office now and see if Ken has one available?"

"Whatever you want, my million-dollar bride." He reached for the door handle. "Cabin 5?"

"Any cabin is fine with me . . . as long as you can't escape out the window."

"Check my planner," he said, smiling. "I have no plans to escape from you for at least the next fifty years. Of course, you realize, you won't be allowed to escape from me, either."

"Sounds like heaven." She kissed him thoroughly. "Maybe you should hurry and get the key to the cabin before I start thinking how much I like kissing you in the nude." She nudged him toward the door. "Go. Please. And don't forget to take Ken's clothes."

He reached over the seat and picked up a new pair of jeans and a crisp new shirt. "Got them." He opened the car door and stepped out, only to lean down and look at her. "Now, don't talk to strangers while I'm in the office, and whatever you do, don't get out of this car and start thumbing a ride out of town."

She watched Mack walk around the front of the car and enter the office of the Hay Capitol Motel. She could hardly believe she was his wife. What an extraordinary, incredible bit of... She thought of the million-dollar dress again. "Magic," she whispered to the stars. "What a beautiful bit of magic."

A couple of sharp taps on the window startled her, and she turned to see the twin frowns of Sheriff and Deputy Cooper. Rolling down the window, she readied an explanation for her and Mack's abrupt departure from town. "Hello," she said brightly. "I'll bet you didn't expect to see Mack and me back so soon."

Tim looked at Jim... or vice versa. "Well, now, I reckon we didn't, but when I saw you two sittin' in this car, neckin' for the whole town to see, I said to the sheriff here, 'the nuc'es are back.'"

"We're on our honeymoon. We're driving to Denver and then catching a plane to Hawaii. But we wanted to spend another night here. Mack has just gone inside to take back the clothes he borrowed from your cousin and to see if we can have Cabin 5.''

"I'm sure Ken can arrange it,'' one of the twins drawled. ''And if the cabins are full, you can always have adjoining cells down at the jail.''

Her eyes widened and the lawmen laughed...in unison, of course.

"Don't worry, Mrs. Cortland, we don't want you and your husband cluttering up our jail. Besides, as it happens, we sort of owe you and Mack a thank-you.''

"You do?''

Mack came out of the office and paused briefly when he saw who was standing beside the car. ''Sheriff Cooper,'' he said with a polite nod. ''Deputy Cooper. Nice to see you again.''

"You, too, Mack.'' Deputy Cooper touched the brim of his hat, while Sheriff Cooper adjusted his belt buckle. ''We were just tellin' Eliza here that we want to thank you for jumpin' bail like you did and leavin' me locked in the cabin. I bet you thought that was pretty clever.''

"I thought it was pretty funny,'' the twin with the sheriff's badge said.

"Yeah, well, it wasn't too funny at the time, but everythin' worked out darn good.'' The deputy twin smiled broadly at Eliza. ''Mack told me I was wanted on the phone inside the cabin, and when I went in to answer it, he latched the door. Now, we haven't figured out why the two of you ran off like you did, but we have to tell ya that because of that phone call we got hooked up with two sisters who look enough alike to be twins.''

"They look like Madonna and cook like the Pillsbury Dough Boy." The sheriff looped his thumb through a belt loop. "Yep, me and Tim are feeling darn good and very forgivin', if you get my meaning."

"Meaning we can enjoy our honeymoon and complimentary breakfast at the Sunflower Café without any interference from the law?"

"That's right, but we'd appreciate the two of you staying away from Miz Vangie's farm this evening. We got ourselves a hot date and don't want it interrupted by gettin' called out to investigate two nudies in a haystack."

"You don't have a thing to worry about." Mack opened the car door and got in before holding up a motel key for display. "Eliza and I are on our honeymoon, and I assure you that we're not going anywhere near that haystack."

"Don't give us a second thought," she said. "We're going to be busy watching each other not sleep."

Smiling, Mack put the car into gear as she rolled up the window and waved. They drove away from the office and the twin sheriffs and coasted down the gravel drive to Cabin 5.

"I've been thinking, Mack."

He raised his eyebrows.

"Not about the dress. You're right about that. It's safely stored and out of our hands, even if that spacey little laundry clerk takes it into her head to try it on. I mean, even if she does, the worst that could happen is she might fall in love and live happily ever after, right? So I've decided it's silly to think about the million-dollar dress anymore. But I was sort of thinking about the haystack and—''

''We are not spending the night in that haystack, Eliza,'' he said firmly.

''No, I didn't think you'd want to do that, but you know Jake and Tamra eloped over the weekend, and they won't be using the old barn anymore, and I was thinking that maybe we could get a tablecloth and go out there and, well, you know....''

Mack parked the car in the shadowed darkness near the cabin, cupped his hand at the back of her head and drew her close. ''There are certain family traditions you will have to live with from now on, Eliza. One of them is that Cortland heirs are conceived in beds, not haystacks, and certainly not in barns.''

''Oh. Well, then, the answer is obvious. When we go out there, we'll take along a broom for protection.''

He looked at her as if he didn't know whether to argue or kiss her. So she curled her arms around his neck and snuggled into his arms. ''You have a lot to learn about being married to me, Mr. Cortland.'' She kissed him long and persuasively, and coaxed him down onto the car seat. ''Lucky for you, I am very good with explanations.''

BRIDE'S BAY RESORT

UNLOCK THE DOOR TO GREAT ROMANCE AT BRIDE'S BAY RESORT

Join Harlequin's new across-the-lines series, set in an exclusive hotel on an island off the coast of South Carolina.

Seven of your favorite authors will bring you exciting stories about fascinating heroes and heroines discovering love at Bride's Bay Resort.

Look for these fabulous stories coming to a store near you beginning in January 1996.

Harlequin American Romance #613 in January
Matchmaking Baby by Cathy Gillen Thacker

Harlequin Presents #1794 in February
Indiscretions by Robyn Donald

Harlequin Intrigue #362 in March
Love and Lies by Dawn Stewardson

Harlequin Romance #3404 in April
Make Believe Engagement by Day Leclaire

Harlequin Temptation #588 in May
Stranger in the Night by Roseanne Williams

Harlequin Superromance #695 in June
Married to a Stranger by Connie Bennett

Harlequin Historicals #324 in July
Dulcie's Gift by Ruth Langan

Visit Bride's Bay Resort each month wherever Harlequin books are sold.

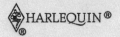

HARLEQUIN ®

BBAYG

Once in a while, there's a story so special, a story so unusual,
that your pulse races, your blood rushes. We call this

TWIST OF FATE is one such story.

Though she was slinging hash in a two-bit diner, Allie Walker had dreams of
grandeur. And of P.I. Pete Hackett. But when her dreams came true, they seemed
more like a nightmare. After being shot, she was somehow switched into the body
of beautiful socialite Brianne Sinclair! Only problem is, there's a dead man at her
feet and Brianne is holding the smoking gun. Now she needs Pete in more than just
a physical way!

#627 TWIST OF FATE
by
Linda Randall Wisdom
April 1996

Don't miss this Heartbeat title—it's Linda Randall Wisdom's 50th book!

"TWIST OF FATE is pure magic!"

—Harriet Klausner, *Affaire de Coeur*

HEART11

HARLEQUIN®

AMERICAN ◆ ROMANCE®
®

In Name Only

...because there are many reasons for saying "I do."

American Romance cordially invites you to a
wedding of convenience. This is one reluctant bride
and groom with their own unique reasons for
marrying...IN NAME ONLY.

By popular demand American Romance continues this
story of favorite marriage-of-convenience books. Don't
miss

#624 THE NEWLYWED GAME
by Bonnie K. Winn
March 1996

Find out why some couples marry first...and learn to
love later. Watch for IN NAME ONLY!

INO

The Magic Wedding Dress

Imagine a wedding dress that costs a million dollars.
Imagine a wedding dress that allows the wearer to
find her one true love—not always the man she
thinks it is. And then imagine a wedding dress that
brings out all the best attributes in its bride, so that
every man who glimpses her is sure to fall in love.
Karen Toller Whittenburg imagined just such a dress
and allowed it to take on a life of its own in her new
American Romance trilogy, *The Magic Wedding Dress*.
Be sure to catch all three:

March
#621—THE MILLION-DOLLAR BRIDE

May
#630—THE FIFTY-CENT GROOM

August
#643—THE TWO-PENNY WEDDING

Come along and dream with Karen Toller Whittenburg!

HARLEQUIN®
AMERICAN ✦ ROMANCE®

*With only forty-eight hours to lasso their mates—
it's a stampede...to the altar!*

WILD WEST
Weddings

by Cathy Gillen Thacker

Looking down from above, Montana maven
Max McKendrick wants to make sure his heirs get
something money can't buy—true love! And if his two
nephews and niece want to inherit their piece of his
sprawling Silver Spur ranch then they'll have to wed the
spouse of *his* choice—within forty-eight hours!

Don't miss any of the Wild West Weddings titles!

Yo amo novelas con corazón!

Starting this March, Harlequin opens up to a whole new world of readers with two new romance lines in SPANISH!

Harlequin Deseo
- passionate, sensual and exciting stories

Harlequin Bianca
- romances that are fun, fresh and very contemporary

With four titles a month, each line will offer the same wonderfully romantic stories that you've come to love—now available in Spanish.

Look for them at selected retail outlets.

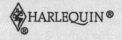 HARLEQUIN®

Fall in love all over again with

This Time...
MARRIAGE

In this collection of original short stories, three brides
get a unique chance for a return engagement!

- Being kidnapped from your bridal shower by a
  one-time love can really put a crimp in your
  wedding plans! *The Borrowed Bride*—
  by **Susan Wiggs**, *Romantic Times* Career
  Achievement Award-winning author.

- After fifteen years a couple reunites for the sake
  of their child—this time will it end in marriage?
  The Forgotten Bride—by **Janice Kaiser.**

- It's tough to make a good divorce stick—especially
  when you're thrown together with your ex in a
  magazine wedding shoot! *The Bygone Bride*—
  by **Muriel Jensen.**

Don't miss THIS TIME...MARRIAGE, available in
April wherever Harlequin books are sold.

HARLEQUIN ®

BRIDE96